DEFYING CONVENTION

WOMEN WHO CHANGED THE RULES

WOMEN POLITICAL LEADERS

ANNE C. CUNNINGHAM

Enslow Publishing
101 W. 23rd Street
Suite 240
New York, NY 10011
USA

enslow.com

Published in 2017 by Enslow Publishing, LLC.
101 W. 23rd Street, Suite 240, New York, NY 10011

Library of Congress Cataloging-in-Publication Data

Names: Cunningham, Anne C., author.
Title: Women political leaders / Anne C. Cunningham.
Description: New York City : Enslow Publishing, 2017. | Series: Defying convention: women who changed the rules | Includes bibliographical references and index.
Identifiers: LCCN 2016032316 | ISBN 9780766081413 (library bound)
Subjects: LCSH: Women heads of state—Juvenile literature. | Women cabinet officers—Juvenile literature. | Women—Political activity—Juvenile literature.
Classification: LCC HQ1236 .C86 2017 | DDC 320.082—dc23
LC record available at https://lccn.loc.gov/2016032316

Printed in Malaysia

To Our Readers: We have done our best to make sure all websites in this book were active and appropriate when we went to press. However, the author and the publisher have no control over and assume no liability for the material available on those websites or on any websites they may link to. Any comments or suggestions can be sent by e-mail to customerservice@enslow.com.

Photo Credits: Cover (top left), p. 112 Drew Angerer/Getty Images; cover (top right), p. 73 Library of Congress Prints and Photographs Division; cover (bottom left) Dimitrios Kambouris/Getty Images; cover (bottom right), pp. 46, 68 Everett - Art/Shutterstock.com; p. 5, 53, 60 Heritage Images/Hulton Fine Art Archive/Getty images; p. 10 Vladimir Wrangel/Shutterstock.com; pp. 14, 31, 44 Print Collector/Hulton Archive/Getty Images; pp. 18, 23, 56 De Agostini Picture Library/Getty Images; p. 26 Universal History Archive/Universal Images Group/Getty Images; p. 28 DEA/G. Dagli Orti/De Agostini/Getty Images; p. 37 Arena Photo UK/Shutterstock.com; pp. 40, 70 Everett Historical/Shutterstock.com; p. 42 Imagno/Hulton Fine Art Collection/Getty Images; p. 51 Culture Club/Hulton Archive/Getty Images; p. 65 SuperStock/Getty Images; p. 79 Fotosearch/Archive Photos/Getty Images; p. 85 Keystone/Hulton Archive/Getty Images; p. 88 Eric Feferberg/AFP/Getty Images; p. 92 Bettmann/Getty Images; p. 96 Jean Guichard/Gamma-Rapho/Getty Images; p. 100 Amanda Edwards/WireImage/Getty Images; p. 104 © AP Images; p. 107 Veronique de Viguerie/Getty Images News

CONTENTS

INTRODUCTION

With very few exceptions, human social groups have historically recognized the expediency of selecting leaders. In early societies, the doctrine of "might-makes-right" meant that most of these leaders were male. In the aftermath of decisive battles, distinguished warriors ruled over their people and vanquished foes. Owing to the greater physical strength men generally (but not always) possess, these leaders were, more often than not, men.

Gradually, brains became more important than brawn as the main qualification for leadership. As raw muscle diminished in primacy relative to social status, intelligence, and political acumen, we might expect to see the frequency of female leadership reflect the roughly equivalent number of men and women comprising most populations. We would be dead wrong. Long after the age of the warrior-king, male dominance was institutionalized as patriarchy. This term refers to social systems ensuring that power stays concentrated in the hands of men. Lines of succession favoring sons are the most literal example of patriarchal power. However, other less visible factors such as the ideology of male privilege and the systemic repression of women's rights have also been essential in the maintenance of this social order and account for the far fewer examples of women political leaders. The very fact that

Examples of women political leaders, such as eighteenth-century Russian empress Catherine the Great, are rare.

a book on women political leaders exists foregrounds this dearth.

Despite persistent patterns of male dominance, women do in fact occupy the highest offices of their respective societies, and they have since ancient times. However, due to patriarchy, instances of female rule are typically marked by complex negotiations of gender identity. For example, in ancient Egypt, queens such as Hatshepsut were depicted with beards and sometimes even shown smiting enemies in battle. This was not an attempt to fool subjects into thinking

Hatshepsut was male. Rather, through masculine aesthetic representations, the perceived power of the pharaoh's office was preserved and reinforced. In this sense, the presence of an individual female ruler is rendered distinct from disembodied patriarchal power. The "power-dressing" pantsuit style favored by contemporary politicians such as Margaret Thatcher and Hillary Clinton are part of this lineage. By adapting signifiers of dress associated with masculinity, these women leaders project authority that a traditional performance of femininity would perhaps undermine.

Nuanced and skillful navigation of male birthright is another relative constant among female political figures in their rise to leadership. Under monarchy, power is hereditary. Therefore, securing an advantageous match through marriage is one important pathway through which women have ascended to power under monarchies. Catherine the Great was not even born in Russia, yet she is Russia's most important queen. She became queen through her mother's exploitation of fairly tenuous social ties, and after a period of "leading from behind" (also typical of female leaders), she gradually assumed control of the nation, exerting a modernizing force. Other leaders such as Catherine de Medici expanded their political power through periods of acting as regents in the stead of a male heir to power either too young or disinterested to assume the throne.

In addition to the legendary queens and empresses found throughout history, we also find women playing leading roles as activists, agents of political change, and leaders of social progress across the globe. Harriet Tubman risked her life countless times in her efforts as an abolitionist and "conductor" of the Underground Railroad. More recently, Malala Yousafzai began speaking up about girls' education, causing the Taliban to attempt an assassination on a mere twelve-year-old. These instances of bravery and outspokenness are even more meaningful coming from a woman, as women are not supposed to be outspoken in traditional, religiously dominated societies. There is evidence that through the actions of these courageous leaders, this can and will change.

While some leaders such as Theodora of Constantine advocated for women's rights, there is in fact no logical or necessary link between female leadership and advocacy for actual females. In reality however, the instances in which female leaders have demonstrated solidarity with their female subjects greatly outnumber examples to the contrary. While we would urge resistance to essentialist terms such as "female leadership style," the historical tendency of female leaders to be comparatively inclusive should not be ignored either. If history provides a credible model for the future, growing numbers of women in positions of leadership worldwide will bode well for the broadening of human rights and equality.

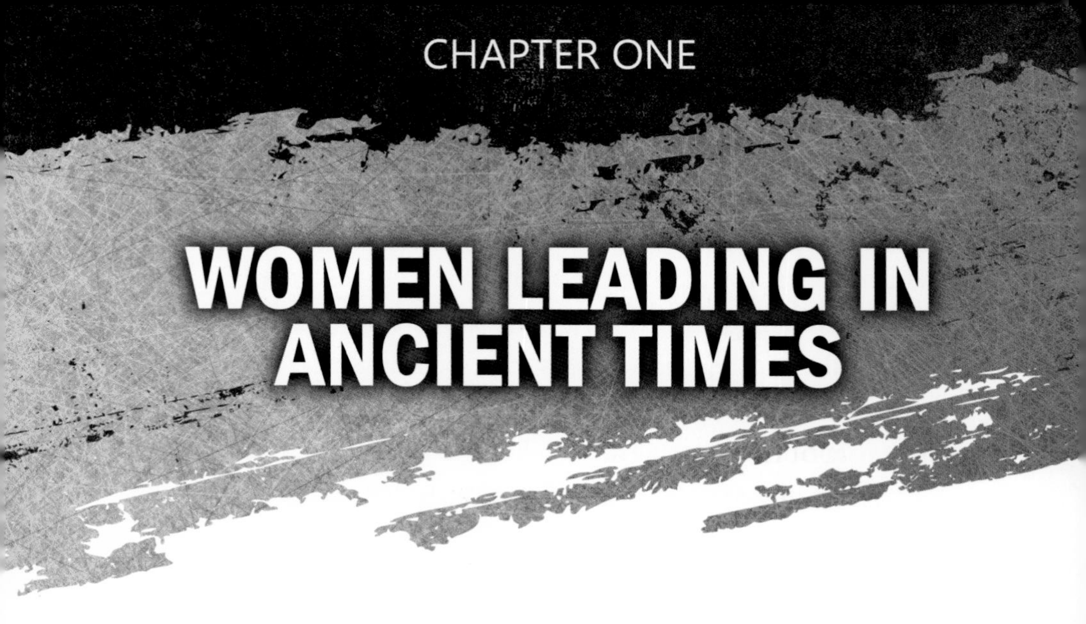

CHAPTER ONE

WOMEN LEADING IN ANCIENT TIMES

The ancient world begins roughly five thousand years ago with the development of Sumerian cuneiform writing and ends with the fall of the Roman Empire in 476 CE. Multiple advanced civilizations such as Mesopotamia and Persia existed during this time, located in what we now call North Africa and the Middle East. However, it is in ancient Egypt where we find the most notable and interesting examples of female leadership. The lives and careers of famous female Egyptian leaders such as Nefertiti, Hatshepsut, and Cleopatra are exemplary of how gender and sexuality intersected with political power in this corner of the ancient world.

Although women enjoyed a relatively high status and quality of life in ancient Egypt, it was still very much a male-dominated society. Thus, female pharaohs were relatively few and far between. Scholars believe this is the reason why women leaders were frequently depicted with beards and weapons. Since political power and masculinity were inextricably linked in the ancient consciousness, influential artists aligned female leaders such as Hatshepsut with these typically masculine signifiers. This was not to fool the public into thinking these women were in fact men, but rather to maintain the perceived power of the pharaoh's office. With Queen Nefertiti, this practice also coincided with the veneration of her feminine beauty. This created an oscillation of gender ideals—in this case, embodied in one individual woman.

Cleopatra famously held power while ancient Egypt came under Grecian rule and eventual decline. Although it is commonly believed that Cleopatra used her sexuality as a tool to maintain political power, a look at her story and tragic end reveals a continuous navigation of complex historical circumstances and expectations rather than simple opportunism.[1]

QUEEN NEFERTITI (CA. 1370–1330 BCE)

Queen Nefertiti was a legendary Egyptian queen and the wife of pharaoh Akhenaten during the fourteenth century BCE. Literally translated, Nefertiti means "the beautiful one who has

Queen Nefertiti, still held up as a female beauty ideal, ruled Egypt with her husband, the pharoah Akhenaten. The couple maneuvered a religious shift throughout their land and were responsible for other cultural influences as well.

come,"[2] and by all accounts she lived up to this name. Representations of Nefertiti remain enduring signifiers of universal beauty, arguably due to their merger of noble traits previously associated with either femininity or masculinity into one singular and sublime embodiment.

Queen Nefertiti and Akhenaten's eighteen-year reign coincided with a very prosperous period in ancient Egyptian history. Diverging from, and perhaps innovating upon, the traditional polytheism of ancient Egypt, the couple established a new religious cult based around worship of the sun god Aten to the exclusion of all other gods. Their relationship influenced the aesthetics of the day as well. They promoted art that displayed a novel and more naturalistic approach, as well as a more fluid understanding of gender. Surviving representative works from this period depict the couple as lovers and equals, which was unusual in the ancient world. One such work, the bust of Nefertiti located in the German Neues Museum, ranks among the most iconic works of art of ancient Egypt—if not the entire ancient world. The royal couple had six daughters before Nefertiti eventually disappeared from all depictions and public life. Nefertiti's sudden disappearance adds yet another layer of mystery to her fabled existence.

Nefertiti's precise origin is the subject of much conjecture and is still not known for certain. Some scholars believe she was related to (possibly even the daughter of) the pharaoh Ay. Others speculate she arrived in Egypt from a neighboring country, most likely Syria. However, evidence now suggests that she was most likely Egyptian due to her having an Egyptian wet nurse.

Nefertiti and Akhenaten (then known as Amenhotep IV) were married when she was about fifteen years old. Based on artistic depictions, Nefertiti was seen as a powerful figure from the outset. In addition to depictions of Nefertiti supporting her husband in his duties as king, she was also represented in stereotypically masculine ways, such as wearing a crown or victoriously battling against enemies.

Four years into her reign as queen, Nefertiti changed her name to Neferneferuaten-Nefertiti, meaning, "The Aten is radiant of radiance (because) the beautiful one has come."[3] This name change was not intended as self-aggrandizement, which would have been unnecessary. Rather, it was an attempt to support her husband's growing immersion in his monotheistic religious philosophy centered around worship of the sun god Aten. Against much popular resistance, the couple worked hard to convert common Egyptians to this worldview, efforts that might be described as "evangelical" in the extreme today. For example, they ordered the closing of temples to other gods and moved the capital city to a remote location. Furthermore, common people were told that they could only access Aten through the royal couple, a difficult feat considering the couple's retreat to a faraway corner of Egypt. While some historians see Atenism as a precursor to Judeo-Christian religious thought and the royal couple promoting this as prophets, others argue that despite superficial similarity, the two worldviews are not easily reconciled.

Fourteen years into the couple's rule, Nefertiti suddenly disappeared. Her whereabouts are still a mystery, as no mummy or tomb has ever been located. Theories abound suggesting that Nefertiti became a coregent and changed her gender, assuming the name Smenkhkare and living out the rest of her life disguised as a man. Others think the royal couple had a falling out. In this scenario, the king ordered Nefertiti to be banished, or worse. A less dramatic view holds that Nefertiti died of natural causes or illness but was spared immortalizing with a discreet, secret burial.

HATSHEPSUT (1507–1458 BCE)

Hatshepsut, meaning "foremost of noble ladies" ruled over Egypt for twenty years as the fifth pharaoh of the Eighteenth Dynasty of Egypt. She was the longest reigning female pharaoh and is considered by historians of ancient Egypt to have been

This Egyptian sculpture depicts Queen Hatshepsut with a ceremonial beard. The fifth pharoah of Egypt's Eighteenth Dynasty, she enjoyed a reign of two decades.

the earliest, most politically competent, and most successful queens of the ancient world.[4]

Devotees of the TV drama *Game of Thrones* will find Hatshepsut's story curiously familiar. Hatshepsut was born in the year 1507 BCE. She was the daughter of Egyptian king Thutmose I and his primary wife, Ahmose. Due to this lineage, Hatshepsut was in line to be queen. At age twelve, she married her half brother Thutmose II, immediately following the death of their father, Thutmose I. Although they shared a father, Thutmose II was the son of Mutnofret, another woman of high birth and royal descent. Hatshepsut and Thutmose II had one daughter, Neferure, and Thutmose II also fathered a son, Thutmose III, with a concubine named Iset.

Thutmose II died after a fairly unremarkable fifteen-year reign as king. It is assumed that Hatshepsut exerted much influence over her husband during this time. Thus, when she became a widow at age thirty, she was already the de facto queen. However, ancient Egypt was indeed a patriarchy. Since Hatshepsut had a daughter but no sons, the couple had no legitimate heir to the throne. Thus, Thutmose III officially became ruler of the nation, despite his mother's comparatively low social status. Since he was obviously too young to rule, Hatshepsut acted as regent in his stead. Her ascent was one year after the young child became the (future) ruler of Egypt.

After seven years in the coregent role, Hatshepsut "promoted" herself from queen to pharaoh. She did this with the full support of the military, as well as her former coruler Thutmose III. At this time she began the practice of having herself depicted in male garb. This was not a rearrangement of her individual gender identity but a projection of the power of her office. Her association with masculine signifiers was meant to project an image of strength and align her office with power in the eyes of her subjects.

Rulers of ancient Egypt typically either chose to conquer new territory or secure borders and build prosperity, as well as monuments to such prosperity, at home. Hatshepsut hewed to the latter path. She eschewed any expansionist policies in favor of spreading financial and aesthetic wealth around her nation. To this end, she commissioned the construction of a new temple called Djeser-djeseru, meaning "holiest of holy places." She also established advantageous trade practices and networks. One interesting expedition, to the land of Punt, holds the distinction of being the first successful international transplanting of trees. Other desirable goods, such as frankincense and myrrh, were brought back for the enjoyment of her countrymen.

Hatshepsut died in 1458 BCE. The cause of death was most likely a toxic salve that she used to ameliorate a congenital skin condition.

She left behind an impressive record of nation building and public works. Despite these achievements, her successor, Thutmose III, was responsible for defacing her memory to some extent. However, scholars believe that this was an assertion of his line of succession, not a personal attack on Hatshepsut's legacy.

CLEOPATRA (69–30 BCE)

Cleopatra VII Philopater, better known simply as Cleopatra, was the last pharaoh of Ptolemaic Egypt. She is legendary for inserting sexuality into politics, forging affairs with foreign leaders such as Julius Ceasar and later Mark Antony to retain her grip on power in Egypt. Although this is true on the surface, historians suggest that it would have required more than feminine charms to rule as long and as competently as she did. Those that make Cleopatra's name synonymous with opportunism miss an important part of her individual character, as well as the shifting dynamics and context of the ancient milieu in which her life was situated.

Cleopatra ruled over Ptolemaic Egypt from 51 BCE to the Roman conquest of Egypt in 30 BCE. Ptolemaic Egypt was a period during which Egypt was ruled by the Ptolemaic dynasty, a clan of Macedonian Greeks. The Ptolemaic dynasty ran territories conquered by Alexander the Great

By the time Cleopatra assumed the throne, it was inevitable that Egypt would fall to the Roman Empire. Her test would be in forging relations with Rome.

during his many successful military campaigns across the Mediterranean and North Africa. These years of Greek colonial rule are commonly referred to as the Hellenistic period and lasted from 323 BCE to 31 BCE. At this time, the Roman Empire assumed control over Ptolemaic Egypt, signaling the end of the Hellenistic period and the emergence of the Roman Empire.[5]

Cleopatra was a direct descendent of Ptolemy I, the original ruler of Egypt after the conquest of Alexander the Great. Ptolemy I, II, and III retained a strong sense of Greek identity and did not learn much Egyptian language or culture. However, by the time Cleopatra assumed the throne, she not only learned the language, but also cast herself as the reincarnation of the god Isis. This merging of identities, or blatant act of cultural appropriation depending on one's viewpoint, did much to secure Cleopatra's eventual power.

The Hellenistic period was something of a cultural high point in ancient Greece, but it also had a degenerative undercurrent. While learning, the arts, and exploration flourished to some degree, the early Ptolemaic rulers also sanctioned inequality and wealth redistribution from the common people to the Greek ruling class. This was especially true in Egypt. By the time Cleopatra and her brothers (one of whom she was married to) jointly assumed the throne from their father

Ptolemy XII, the writing was already on the wall that the Roman Empire would inevitably assume rule over Egypt. Although the Ptolemaic dynasty was wealthy, they were decadent and lacked the military prowess of the ascendant Roman Empire. For this reason, Cleopatra's tenure was structured by the eventuality of decline. Her genius was in the negotiation of this situation.

Cleopatra took full control over the throne primarily due to her age difference with her brother, and now husband, who was much younger and whom she did not see as an equal. Her term as pharaoh started off smoothly but was soon plagued by problems such as a flood of the Nile and famines. A larger problem was conflict with Roman troops stationed in Alexandria, which forced Cleopatra to flee Egypt. She was famously smuggled to the palace of Julius Caesar, rolled in a large carpet. The two had a son, Caesarion, and with Caesar's help Cleopatra was restored to the throne over her brother Ptolemy XIV. At this point however, Alexandria was very unstable.

Cleopatra spent much time with Caesar in his Roman country estate. She was there when Caesar was assassinated in 44 BCE. The ensuing power struggle left Rome weak. To raise cash and support, Mark Antony journeyed to Egypt to summon Cleopatra. After an ostentatious courtship the two became lovers and were married in 35 BCE. The marriage severed Antony's ties to Rome. The two would become collateral damage of alliances too complex to chronicle here, and they eventually took their own lives in what was perhaps history's most famous double suicide.

While Cleopatra's life story is to some degree coextensive with her notable Roman partners, she was also a fearsome intellect and allegedly understood nine languages without a translator. Moreover, her social graces and wit were beyond reproach. Doubtless if she was born into a more stable social world her life might not have had such tragic contours. Then again, as evidenced by Shakespeare's *Antony and Cleopatra*, her tragedy and downfall is inseparable with her status as one of the most notable female figures in world history.[6]

CHAPTER TWO

WOMEN LEADERS OF THE MIDDLE AGES

When we think of the Middle Ages, we usually conjure images of knights in shining armor and legendary medieval kings. Indeed, most women in the Middle Ages were excluded from political life and relegated to the domestic sphere. Yet this period, broadly defined as the time from the fifth to the fifteenth centuries CE, did see a few monarchs and important leaders who were women. Those who came to power in this period generally did so through wealth and family connections, though there were exceptions to this.

One such outlier was Theodora of Constantinople. Constantinople was a large city on the eastern edge of Europe. When Theodora rose to power in the sixth century, it was also the wealthiest city in Europe. Although Theodora did not come from great wealth, she was able to parlay her fame as a performer into a marriage with the emperor

Women's roles in the Middle Ages centered around domestic life. They were responsible for caring for the family and the home. It was nearly unheard of that a woman would be a leader, much less a political leader.

Justinian. Together, they ruled over a turbulent time, and Theodora was Justinian's most trusted advisor. Theodora was also something of a proto-feminist as well. She ended forced prostitution, closed brothels, and loosened harsh punishments on adulterous wives.

By contrast, Eleanor of Aquitaine came from great wealth. Interestingly, she played a major role in shaping medieval culture through her famous Court of Love, which taught ideals of chivalry and disseminated these ideas throughout the world, as she is believed to have inspired the very popular literary genre of courtly love.

THEODORA OF CONSTANTINOPLE (CA. 497–548)

Born in Constantinople (Istanbul, Turkey, today) in 497, Theodora became a Byzantine empress after marrying the emperor Justinian, who reigned from 527 to 565. Theodora was arguably the most powerful woman in Byzantine history. Her great intelligence and political skills not only made her Justinian's most trusted advisor, but also enabled her to use her office to promote the religious and social policies that she found important. Though not much is certain or written about her early life, Procopius of Caesarea's colorful book *Secret History* writes that her father, Acacius, was a bear keeper at the

Hippodrome (a closed circus connected to the palace) in Constantinople and her mother was a dancer. Theodora's father died when she was a young girl, and her mother presented her to the Hippodrome, where she was forced to support her sisters and worked as an actress. Theodora earned a living by using her theatrical and sexual skills, apparently making a name for herself with a scintillating performance of "Leda and the Swan." She traveled to North Africa and was away from Constantinople for four years.

Theodora returned to Constantinople in 522, where she gave up her wild lifestyle and settled down to become a wool spinner in a small house near the palace. Her beauty, wit, colorful character, and charm attracted Justinian, who at the time was heir to the throne of his uncle, Emperor Justin I, and she soon became his mistress. The couple wanted to wed, but there was a Roman law preventing the marriage of government officials to actresses. Justinian asked his aunt, Empress Euphemia, to change the law on his behalf. Euphemia was known to grant her nephew special favors, but due to Theodora's scandalous reputation and her former profession, she refused this request and fought to keep the law to prevent their marriage. The couple remained together but unwed for three years, until 525 when Euphemia died. Justinian then finally repealed the law and married Theodora legally, who by this point had a daughter out of wedlock; it is not clear if Justinian was the

Byzantine empress Theodora was the wife of Emperor Justinian I. The couple was so revered that they are saints in the Eastern Orthodox religion. Theodora was widely considered to be the braver and better leader.

biological father of the daughter (name unknown) but he did treat her as his own.

Theodora became empress once Justinian assumed control of Byzantium in 527. Theodora wielded considerable influence, and many believed she was far more active in political affairs than her husband. Her name is mentioned in nearly all the laws passed during the time of their reign. Theodora received foreign envoys and negotiated with other rulers of great import, activities of governing that are conventionally reserved for the emperor. Her influence proved to be particularly crucial during the Nika revolt of 532. Two main political factions in Constantinople, the blues and the greens, had many grievances and united in their opposition to overthrow Justinian, seeking to replace him with a rival emperor, Hypatius. The riot began during a chariot race in the Hippodrome, and soon rioters set out to destroy property and public buildings by setting them on fire. As the mob grew out of control, Justinian's advisors and officials prepared to flee, but Theodora urged them against running, extolling the nobility of royalty. She was determined to stay, stating she would rather die a ruler than live in exile. Her speech convinced Justinian and the other members of the council who were planning to escape. Justinian then ordered his troops, led

The Nika revolt began at a chariot race in the Hippodrome, as shown in this relief. During the riots, it was Theodora who convinced Justinian to stand his ground, rather than flee.

by the trusted general Belisarius, to attack the demonstrators, killing more than thirty thousand people, including Hypatius, at Theodora's insistence. Most historians agree that it was Theodora's ambition and drive that allowed for Justinian's reign, and that Justinian himself never forgot it was Theodora who had secured his throne.

After the riots, great improvements were made as Justinian and Theodora repaired and rebuilt Constantinople. They rebuilt more than twenty-five churches, the grandest being the Hagia Sophia, which is considered one of the architectural wonders of the world. Yet despite these improvements, the imperial couple became feared as rulers. They would have visitors, even government officials, go through much trouble and discomfort to see them. Theodora created her own centers of power at the Hagia Sophia and was very active in legal and spiritual reforms. She is best known for her involvement with the rights of women. Theodora passed laws that prohibited forced prostitution and closed brothels. She expanded the rights of women in divorce and property ownership and instituted the death penalty for rape, gave mothers guardianship rights over their children, and removed the death penalty for wives who committed adultery.

Theodora died of cancer at age forty-eight, yet her influence was so strong that Justinian continued to defend her causes after her death. Theodora has captured the imagination of artists and writers throughout the centuries. She has been portrayed in many famous paintings, films, historical novels, plays, and even video games.[1]

ELEANOR OF AQUITAINE (CA. 1122–1204)

Born in 1122 in southern France, Eleanor was one of the most powerful and wealthiest women during the Middle Ages. As Duchess of Aquitaine, she inherited a tremendous fortune at the age of fifteen, making her a famously sought-after bride. She would become both the queen of France and England, lead an unsuccessful crusade to the Holy Land, and influence Western literature with her Court of Love.

Eleanor received an unusually rich education for a girl of her time, thanks to her father, William X, the Duke of Aquitaine. She was steeped in literature, philosophy, and languages, as well as the rules of court life. Her father died when she was fifteen, and she was his sole heir, inheriting her father's title and extensive lands.

Eleanor of Aquitaine was one of the most influential leaders of the Middle Ages and one of the greatest female leaders in world history. The duchess eventually became queen of both France and England.

Because she was so valuable, she was placed under the guardianship of the king of France, and within hours she was betrothed to his son and heir, Louis. The king sent five hundred men to escort Eleanor to meet her new husband and new home. Within three months of becoming duchess, at the young age of fifteen, Eleanor married the soon-to-be King Louis VII of France. The couple had very little time to get to know each other before Louis's father died, making Louis king and Eleanor queen. They were crowned on Christmas Day. Just weeks after her marriage, she found herself living in the Cîté Palace in Paris. Eleanor found the palace unwelcoming, and no expense was spared to suit it to her tastes. Used to the climate in southern France and made uncomfortable by the cold northern drafts, Eleanor is credited with inventing the built-in fireplace, a technology that soon spread throughout Europe.

Their first years as rulers were tumultuous and filled with strife. The king made a series of diplomatic and military blunders that turned his court against him, and he also had a violent conflict with Pope Innocent II that culminated in a massacre of hundreds of innocent people in the small town of Vitry. Due to his guilty conscience over his involvement with the Vitry massacre, Louis and Eleanor agreed to participate in the pope's crusade. It was a dangerous and unsuccessful journey east. The stress of the disastrous venture strained the marriage, and the couple grew estranged. Eleanor sought an annulment soon after, but the pope denied it. She continued to seek the annulment for years, even after the birth of two daughters. The pope finally granted the annulment after increasing public criticism on the grounds of consanguinity—being related by blood—and their two daughters were placed in the custody of the king.

Within two months of her annulment, Eleanor married Henry, the Duke of Normandy. Rumors soon spread that she was having an affair with Henry's father and that she was also related by blood to Henry, but despite these issues the marriage proceeded and the couple were crowned king and queen of England after Henry inherited the throne from King Stephen. This second marriage was far less tumultuous than her first, but Henry and Eleanor were said to argue often, even though they managed to have eight children. Henry was known for his philandering, and although the reasons for the breakdown of their marriage are not entirely documented, it can likely be attributed to Henry's numerous infidelities. While the extent of Eleanor's political influence on the king is unknown, it seems unlikely given her extraordinary education and enthusiasm that she would have none. Yet she did not emerge into a public role until after separating from the king and moving to her own land in Poitiers.

It was during this time, between 1168 and 1173, that Eleanor's influence on shaping the culture was most influential, yet there is very little known about it. Eleanor and her daughters are said to have created a Court of Love to teach ideas of troubadours, chivalry, and courtly love, but the details and impetus of the court are highly debated. Yet it is probable that her Court of Love was a catalyst for the proliferation of tales about knights and courtly love in Western literature, which became a highly popular theme for centuries to follow.

In 1173, Eleanor was arrested and imprisoned for treason. Her son had fled to France and allegedly plotted against his father to seize the English throne. Eleanor was accused of helping her son plan this attack, was apprehended, and spent the next sixteen years in various castles in England under arrest, She was also suspected of plotting against King Henry's interests, as well as playing a part in the death of Rosamund, Henry's beloved mistress. The son continued to rebel for years but fell ill and died in 1183. On his deathbed, he implored the king to release his mother. King Henry agreed and released her, whereupon she resumed ceremonial duties as queen but was still under guard. King Henry died a few years after Eleanor returned, in 1189. Their son Richard inherited the throne, and he fully restored her freedom. Richard left for the Third Crusade, and Queen Eleanor acted as regent while he was away. Eleanor eventually retired as a nun to the abbey at Fontevraud, where she was buried after her death in 1204.[2]

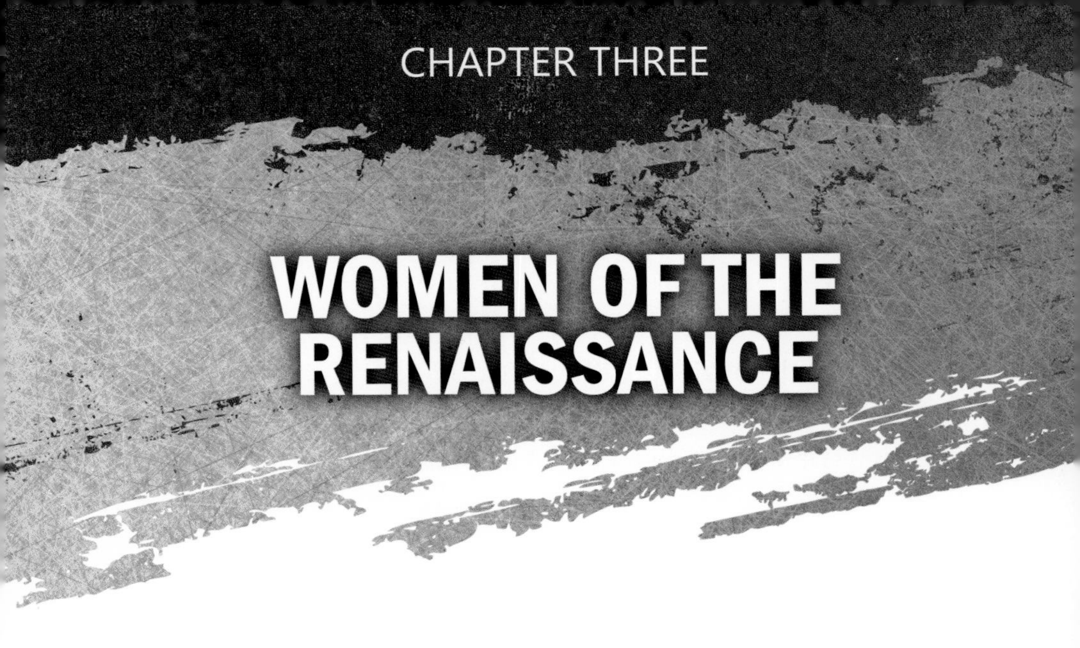

CHAPTER THREE

WOMEN OF THE RENAISSANCE

Like those who preceded them during the Middle Ages, women in the Renaissance generally did not enjoy wide access to the rebirth of learning and public life characteristic of the day. The duties of child rearing and the home remained the chief domain of the vast majority of women. Women of the upper classes did have a greater measure of independence than most, though. Thus, it is from this echelon of society that the period's famous female leaders emerged.

Although female leaders were not common during this time, the few that reigned were disproportionately influential. Queen Elizabeth is one of the most beloved monarchs in English history. Under her rule, England became a top world power over France and Spain. Elizabeth also defied convention by refusing to marry any of her numerous suitors. Similarly, Queen Isabella of Spain charted

enslavement of native people. She was actually among the first vocal advocates for the rights of Native Americans, and she did her best to free slaves from the Spanish colonies. While her efforts would not stem the tide of brutal colonial practices, they are still noteworthy and forward thinking. Her record with regard to Spain's sizeable Jewish population was less commendable. Although she opposed harsh measures against Jews, she presided over the Alhambra Decree, which ordered the expulsion of all Spanish Jews who did not become Catholic converts, or *Conversos*.

Isabella stepped down in 1504 and died later that year. She is remembered as an austere and both fiscally and religiously conservative leader who did much to bolster Spain's power on the international scene.[1]

CATHERINE DE MEDICI (1519–1589)

Catherine de Medici was an Italian noblewoman and, for twelve years, the queen of France. She married King Henry II at the age of fourteen and had three sons, each of whom would be king of France. In love as well as politics, the king favored his mistress, Diane de Poitiers, and excluded Catherine from most important decisions facing the crown. However, once

Catherine de Medici was thrust into a leadership role after the death of her husband, King Henry II of France. During this time, France experienced a series of civil wars known as the French Wars of Religion.

King Henry II died in 1559, Catherine assumed a great deal of influence over French political life. She was widely recognized as the most powerful woman in sixteenth-century France and a competent ruler. Although she presided over a period of great upheaval and conflict, Catherine maintained the stability and integrity of France's state apparatus.

Catherine Maria Romula di Lorenzo de Medici was born is Florence in 1519. Her father, Lorenzo, was a duke of relatively minor social standing, while her mother was related to French royalty. This connection would propel Catherine forward in status once in France. Of course, the de Medici family name was also synonymous with tremendous wealth. Originally bankers, the family was highly successful at this profession, financially backing several of Europe's established monarchies. This bought the family tremendous influence in world affairs.

Both of Catherine's parents died shortly after she was born, leaving Catherine in the charge of her uncle. When Catherine was fourteen, her uncle arranged a match between his niece and the duke of Orleans, who as the king's son was in the line of succession to become king of France, which he assumed in 1544. A subsequent jousting accident would make his reign a short one. Although Catherine and Henry's son Francis

The St. Bartholomew's Day Massacre occurred during the wedding of Catherine's daughter Marguerite and the King of Navarre. Catherine had arranged the union as an attempt at brokering peace.

was next in line to be king, his health was poor. Francis, too, soon died, leaving the crown to his younger brother Charles. Since Charles was only ten years old, this positioned his mother, Catherine, as the acting regent, a role she occupied to the fullest by making all state decisions during this time.

The crown was comparatively weak at this point in French history, as local nobles asserted their own sovereignty. This escalated to civil war with the French Wars of Religion. Much conflict revolved around the Huguenots, French Protestants. In an attempt at extending the olive branch, Catherine brokered a marriage between her daughter Marguerite and the Protestant king of Navarre. Hundreds gathered for the wedding were murdered in what was to become known as the St. Bartholomew's Day Massacre.

In 1574, Charles IX died, promoting Catherine's youngest, healthiest, and favorite son to King Henry III. The two shared power more equitably than she had with the previous two kings. Unfortunately, disorder and civil war still raged throughout France; few of Catherine's efforts at this time were successful in ushering in peace. Catherine died in 1589 and was buried next to her husband.[2]

QUEEN ELIZABETH I (1533–1603)

Queen Elizabeth I was the final monarch of the Tudor dynasty and possibly the preeminent monarch in British history. Although England was less powerful than France and Spain when Elizabeth came to power, she would eventually lead the nation to far greater heights of international

The fifty-year reign of Elizabeth I over England and Ireland was extremely influential. During this time, known as the Elizabethan era, the arts and exploration flourished.

power and prestige. The Tudor period of England, from roughly 1485 to 1603, was a time of rising economic prosperity, territorial expansion, and enduring advances in the arts and literature, such as the works of William Shakespeare. It coincided with a globally ascendant British sphere of influence. Like many so-called golden ages, it was also a time of growing stratification between economic classes, political intrigue, and violence. Queen Elizabeth was a fine temperamental match for this situation. She was lively and sociable, piercingly intelligent, and possessing of a finely honed political instinct.

Elizabeth was born in 1533. Her father, the notorious Henry VIII, desperately wanted Elizabeth to be born male and had dispatched his previous wife, Catherine of Aragon, for bearing girls. A similar fate would befall Elizabeth's mother, Anne Boleyn. When Elizabeth was two years old, Henry ordered Boleyn's beheading. This sentence was based on charges of infidelity and incest that were almost certainly false. Henry subsequently annulled the marriage, rendering young Elizabeth effectively illegitimate. Elizabeth would never have children and was even referred to as "the Virgin Queen." One need not be a psychoanalyst to suspect a link between her father's unconscionably misogynistic murders to Elizabeth's problematic relationship with childbirth.

Although not the son and heir King Henry VIII wished for, Elizabeth's birth was nonetheless a politically charged dramatic event. This was due to the complex politics of succession Henry's many wives and children caused. After the death of her half brother Edward, Elizabeth's cousin Lady Jane Grey became queen. Grey lacked popular support, so Mary (Elizabeth's half sister) easily unseated her after a mere nine days on the throne. As queen, Mary wanted to revert England back to Catholicism, thus erasing her father's dramatic break with the papacy. Elizabeth paid lip service to Mary's intentions but retained enough distance to be seen by Protestants as a viable successor to Queen Mary. On matters of religion, Mary was quite militant. Her ordering of more than three hundred Protestant executions earned her the nickname "Bloody Mary."

Mary died in 1558, leaving Elizabeth the throne, as well as a host of problems. Not only was England divided over religion, it was also engaged in a draining war with France. In response to the former, Elizabeth passed the Act of Supremacy, which restored the Church of England. Glossing over the deep religious divide, Elizabeth established a common set of prayers and practices with the Act of Uniformity.

Militarily, Queen Elizabeth's reign was marked by diplomacy and good fortune. She also ended the war with France and avoided much conflict with Spain. When the Spanish Armada set sail to attack England, the royal navy was able to easily repulse the significant threat. Although the defeat had much to do with the weather, the victory strengthened the nation, as well as Elizabeth's power.

It was assumed that the queen would marry. Although Elizabeth had many suitors, she never chose a spouse. Perhaps she did not want to share power. Also likely, as previously noted, the trauma induced by the plotting, intrigue, and violence marking her upbringing could have made marriage an unappealing prospect. Whatever the ultimate reason, historians agree that this did not slow Elizabeth down one bit. In an environment in which marriage was a basic expectation for women, Elizabeth's assertion of autonomy can be viewed as a proto-feminist stance. Elizabeth I died in 1603, putting an end to the Tudor dynasty.[3]

CHAPTER FOUR

WOMEN LEADING DURING THE ENLIGHTENMENT

The Enlightenment is typically associated with the tradition of rationalism, a philosophical discourse that was primarily the province of male writers. However, beneath the familiar surface of the Enlightenment period, distinctly feminist currents of thought can also be unearthed. Several key female political figures led the way in this emerging paradigm, either as heads of state or influencers of culture.

One important way in which women shaped culture during this time was by establishing salons. Salons provided a forum and opportunity for leading intellectuals and artists to gather. Although women such as Madame de Staël curated and organized the salons, it should be noted that participation in these was restricted to those of the upper classes. Women during this time also held traditional office, too. Catherine the Great was born in Prussia, but under the influence of her mother's connections she was able to secure a marriage to gain control of Russia. Once in power, she exerted a modernizing force over the country, establishing preeminent art museums such as the Hermitage. These institutions catapulted Russia to a leading world power. Mary Wollstonecraft was truly a revolutionary thinker. She published bold pamphlets and books on women's educational reform and sexual rights, hoping to effect change for all women. She was centuries ahead of her time: her *Vindication on the Rights of Women* is still read in college classrooms today.

During the Englightenment, salons allowed the exchange of ideas among elite intellectuals and artists.

MADAME DE STAËL (1776–1817)

Germaine de Staël was a political propagandist, woman of letters, and master conversationalist. The French-Swiss provocateur led a fascinating life. She was exiled from Paris by Napoleon Bonaparte her political views; this exile brought her even more fame and notoriety, making her a subject of fascination across Europe. She epitomized the culture of her time, gaining fame for her salon, which hosted the leading intellectuals of her time. She was a well-regarded author and literary theorist and published numerous writings, including political essays, novels, poems, and a memoir and her literary criticism on Romanticism is still read today.

The daughter of Swiss parents, she was born Anne-Louise Germaine Necker. Her mother introduced her early on to the intellectual and literary life, as she ran a salon to help her husband's political career. Jacque Necker, Germaine's father, was the finance minister to King Louis XVI. Germaine was raised in luxury, thanks to her parents' status and affection. She was also beautiful and soon gained a reputation for her lively wit as well as her physical attributes. Even though a young child, she was invited to her mother's salon, where she would often be seen listening and participating in the lively conversation with some of the nation's leading cultural figures and writers, such as Voltaire and Rousseau. She developed her impressive wit and intellect at an early age, and she maintained her voracious curiosity throughout her life.

At twenty-three, Germaine married Baron Erik de Staël-Holstein, the Swedish ambassador to Paris, but like many upper-class marriages of the time, it was arranged and was not a romantic one. The couple formally separated eleven later.

They did however have three children. A prolific writer, Germaine had written a number of fiction works before she was twenty-one, however she became most known for her nonfiction work, namely her book *Letters on the Works and the Character of J.J. Rousseau* (1788).

Napoleon Bonarparte exiled Anne-Louise Germaine de Staël from Paris because of her influential salon.

Because she was married to a diplomat, de Staël was not in danger during the initial beginning of the French Revolution. Her husband provided diplomatic sanctuary for her and her artistic and literary friends in 1789 when the French Revolution began. Yet during the year of terror, 1793, life in Paris became far too dangerous for de Staël, so she fled to a family chateau in Coppet, Switzerland, near Geneva, and continued to have her salon meetings there. By 1794, order was restored and de Staël returned to Paris, publishing more political essays and resuming her Paris salons. Like her mother before her, she held salons where writers, artists, intellectuals, and critics could discuss their views on politics and literature, while listening to music and appreciating poetry readings as well. Germaine de Staël held one of the most notable salons of the eighteenth century.

Napoleon Bonaparte rose to power in France in 1799, abolishing the monarchy and forming a new government. De Staël's salon had a notable reputation, and as she was always interested in hosting men and women in positions of power, she invited him to attend her famous salon. During their meeting, de Staël and her partner, notable politician and writer of the time Benjamin Constant, shared their political views and ideas, hoping to shape the new government. Yet Napoleon soon grew to despise de Staël and her friends, and he viewed her salon as a liberal resistance group. He also despised Benjamin Constant. Constant had a great influence on de Staël, and it was partly due to him that Bonaparte became so opposed to de Staël. Napoleon felt his own speeches were too similar to those of de Staël, who had published numerous political essays, and wanting to appear original, he banished both de Staël and Constant from Paris.

His extreme act of banishment however backfired in a way, as it quickly drew more attention to de Staël and Constant. The two became quite famous across Europe, the subject of much fascination as they had the power to threaten

Napoleon. De Staël traveled throughout Germany first during her exile in 1803 and was greeted with much fanfare everywhere she went. Her father died, and she returned to Coppet, this time making the chateau headquarters for an anti-Bonaparte movement. She remained in exile, traveling to Italy and eastern Europe, until Napoleon's reign ended. In 1811, while living at Coppet, she married John Rocca, a young army officer. Napoleon fell in 1814, and de Staël moved back to Paris, holding her exclusive salons once again. Lord Byron was a frequent visitor. Sadly, both she and her much younger husband, Rocca, contracted tuberculosis, and her health finally failed her in 1817.[1]

MARY WOLLSTONECRAFT (1759–1797)

Mary Wollstonecraft was a feminist writer and intellectual. Born in London and raised by a violent, abusive father, she left home at an early age. She is most famous for one of the earliest feminist political books written in the effort to reform British patriarchal laws that were unjust for women: *A Vindication of the Rights of Woman*.

Wollstonecraft's father spent his fortune on unsuccessful business and farming ventures. He

Mary Wollstonecraft was a feminist writer and intellectual far ahead of the social mores of her day.

was also abusive. When her mother died in 1780, Mary set out from her home in London to earn her own living. In 1784, she established a school with her sister and close friend, Franny. Franny died in 1785, and unable to manage the school on her own Wollstonecraft took a position as a governess for a wealthy family in Ireland. Her work with the young girls at school however inspired her to write the political pamphlet "Thoughts on the Education of Daughters" in 1787. She also found she was not well suited for domestic work and returned to London to work as a translator and advisor to Joseph Johnson, a noted publisher of radical political texts of the time. Wollstonecraft soon became a regular contributor to his periodical, *The Analytical Review*.

Four years after working with Johnson, she published her most famous work, A *Vindication of the Rights of Woman* (1792). Her book fights against common misconceptions regarding the role of women in society: namely that they must be relegated to the domestic sphere and forced to work only in the home, adding that such unfair confinement creates frustrated mothers and in reaction, they lash out against their children and help. Mary argued for educational reform, demanding that women had the same opportunities for education as men. The book was widely read and, as you can imagine, quite controversial for a time when women had very few legal rights and were considered property of their fathers and then husbands should they enter marriage. Wollstonecraft went on to write *Maria, or the Wrongs of Women*, published in Paris in 1798, a scandalous book arguing that society should recognize and allow for women's sexual desire, a desire she had to assert indeed existed and that it was immoral to stifle. This book was enough to damn her in the eyes of critics.

Understandably, Wollstonecraft was strongly against marriage as an institution. She and her partner, the famous writer and thinker William Godwin, were both feminists. But when she became pregnant in 1797, they decided to wed. Their daughter, Mary, would write the famous novel *Frankenstein* and become the wife of the famous Romantic poet Percy Bysshe Shelley. Sadly, just ten days after giving birth, Wollstonecraft died. Although she died at an early age, Mary Wollstonecraft left her radical mark on society through her political work and writing. *Vindication* is still taught in English and feminist literature courses throughout the country. She was truly a forward thinker, as it wasn't until the next century when women finally gained the right to vote and began to see real progress in terms of gaining equality in a male-dominated society.[2]

CATHERINE THE GREAT (1729–1796)

Catherine the Great was the longest-ruling female emperor of Russia, ruling from 1762 to 1796. Partially owing to her mother's social connections and ambitiousness, she rose up from the lower echelons of upper-class German society to become one of the most renowned leaders in Russian history—of either sex. During her reign, Russia asserted itself as a modernized key player on the European stage, as well as a major world power.

Born Sophia Friederike Auguste, Catherine grew up in Stettin, a city in Prussia that is now the Polish city of Szczecin. Her father was a general from a notable German family, but he was not wealthy. Her mother was eager to use her daughter as a bargaining chip through which to elevate her own status, angling for Catherine to be a contender for future empress of Russia. To accomplish this, she exploited her own fairly weak ties to Russian royalty; her brother was briefly engaged to Elizabeth, empress of Russia, but died before the marriage could happen. The family journeyed to St. Petersburg with the intention of arranging a marriage between Catherine and the empress's nephew and future tsar Peter III (then Peter of Holstein-Gottorp). Although Empress Elizabeth disliked and

Catherine the Great's legacy as a ruler is often overshadowed by her colorful personal life. During her thirty-four-year reign, Russia extended its borders considerably. Catherine also was a champion of the arts and education.

distrusted Catherine's mother, she welcomed her daughter. To her credit, Catherine did much to get in the good graces of the noblewoman, ingratiating herself to the Russian people, learning the language, and even converting from Lutheranism to Russian Orthodox.

Once received by the Russian church, the officially renamed Catherine was clear to marry Peter. In 1745, the bride and groom were only sixteen and seventeen, respectively, but were married with the enthusiastic approval of Peter's aunt Elizabeth. Catherine's father, a staunch Lutheran who opposed his daughter's conversion, did not attend—and presumably did not approve either. Once in power after his aunt's death in 1762, Peter had little wherewithal to rule Russia, a country that he, along with most of Europe, assumed to be a provincial backwater. Perhaps due to this condescending attitude, Peter did not occupy the throne very long. After about six months, Catherine was swiftly installed after a peaceful coup. The transition to power was easy for Catherine. Unlike her husband, she embraced her adopted country and cultivated loyalty and friendship among the nation's influential elite. Surprisingly, her mother's plan had come to fruition without a hitch. Catherine understood that in order for Russia to raise its international profile, it would have to change its image as a cultural wasteland. In these endeavors she was a rousing success. Catherine became a passionate proponent of education and the arts, fostering a dialogue with more aesthetically advanced nations, particularly France. Catherine had a visible role in creating the Imperial Academy of Fine Arts, even laying a foundation stone in 1765. She cultivated friendships with French Enlightenment figures such as Voltaire and Diderot and purchased masterpieces and other artistic treasures that would eventually be collected in the Hermitage, still one of the world's preeminent art museums.

In terms of geopolitics, Catherine the Great was an unapologetic expansionist, and she did so without strain or stress on any of Russia's existing borders. During her rule, the nation annexed much territory, including the strategically important Crimean peninsula accessing the Black Sea and parts of Poland. Unfortunately, her modernization happened faster than Russian peasant culture could adapt. This would become a recurring theme in Russian history, echoed by the later Marxist-Leninist revolutions.

Catherine the Great died of a stroke in 1796. Although some cynical detractors attempted to tarnish her legacy with exaggerated accounts of sexual exploits involving various male consorts, her legacy is beyond reproach given the circumstances. It is now commonly accepted that Catherine the Great, despite whatever human foibles one cares to emphasize, made major advances in Russian politics and culture, paving the way for the nation to become a contemporary superpower.[3]

CHAPTER FIVE

THE VICTORIAN, CIVIL WAR, AND RECONSTRUCTION ERAS

The Victorian era in the United Kingdom is roughly considered to be from about 1837 to 1910. The comparable time period for the United States was the Civil War and Reconstruction eras, which ran from 1861 to 1877, and the post-Reconstruction era, the time that takes us just up to the dawn of the modern Jazz Age, around 1910. Women's roles during this time period in both Europe and in America were characterized by an appalling degree of restrictions. Women could neither own property, vote, nor have the rights to their wages, even though the Industrial Revolution made it necessary for women to work outside of the home.

If women had any power at all, it was strictly relegated to domestic affairs only, and even then, it was usually middle- or upper-class women of leisure who could exercise their limited power of

By the time of the Victorian era, women's lives were restricted to domestic matters. They were not permitted to vote, own property, or control their finances. They were considered the property of men, whether their husbands or fathers.

influence in the public sphere only through their husbands. Under the law, married couples were one entity, and the sole person in power was the husband, who controlled all the money, property, and earnings. Wives were also property of their husbands, which meant that their domestic labor, sexual labor, wages, and children were also property of their husband in the eyes of the law.

Given these horrific sets of circumstances in both Europe and America, it is truly inspiring that there were people like Harriet Tubman, who not only was a woman but also an enslaved woman, to fight for the freedom of the oppressed. Susan B. Anthony, though she did not live long enough to see women earn the right to vote, fought tirelessly her entire life for women's rights. And, although Victorian-era Britain was oppressive to women of all classes, Queen Victoria reigned with much power and persuasion, so much so that her values, tastes, and legacy are still synonymous with much of Britain's culture.

QUEEN VICTORIA (1819–1901)

Queen Victoria was one of the longest-reigning British monarchs in history, serving as queen of England and Ireland as well as the empress of India from 1837 until her death in 1901. Victoria married her first cousin, Prince Albert, in 1840 and had nine children, all of whom married into royal families, earning Victoria the nickname "the grandmother of Europe." Victoria's reign saw unprecedented cultural expansion along with advances in industrialization, science, the arts, and media. The building of the railroad and the London Underground were also completed during her reign.

Victoria was the daughter of Princess Victoria Leiningen of Saxe-Coburg and the Duke of Kent. She was raised with extreme care since birth, since although she was fifth in the line of succession, it seemed likely she would inherit the throne, which she did at age eighteen after the king's three eldest sons died, leaving no surviving children. She was crowned as monarch of the United Kingdom and Ireland in Westminster Abbey in 1838. More than four hundred thousand people lined the streets to show their enthusiasm for the young queen. Victoria became the first ruler to reside at Buckingham Palace. When Victoria took the throne, it was uncertain what role any monarch would continue to play in British politics, as times were changing. Yet under Victoria's rule, Britain made its transition to a constitutional monarchy, ensuring the continuance of the monarchy system for future kings and queens. Victoria's influence on British society ensured the continuance of the crown.

Victoria first met her future husband when she was sixteen. Prince Albert was her first cousin, and Victoria enjoyed his company. Because she was queen, Prince Albert could not propose to her, so she proposed to him when she was eighteen, and they married a year after. Far from many arranged marriages of the time, theirs was a passionate one. Despite her many children, the queen spoke often about the unpleasant effects of what she referred

Queen Victoria was born to the throne, but she allowed herself to be thoroughly influenced by her husband, Albert.

to as the "shadow side of marriage," meaning pregnancy and childbirth. Queen Victoria's relatively unabashed nature was an odd combination with her tiny physical stature; the queen was under 5 feet tall (152 centimeters).

Great Britain, much like the United States, was experiencing unprecedented expansion in industry, and urban centers were evolving rapidly. This was also a time of transition, when great cultural, technological, and scientific change was afoot, ushering in modernism. Charles Darwin's *On the Origin of Species* was published in 1859, and the telegraph and the popular press were changing modes of communication and distributing information to the masses. Britain also expanded its imperial empire through colonization, doubling in size and encompassing Canada, Australia, India, and various countries in Africa and the South Pacific. During this time, Britain experienced very few international conflicts, and this was in part due to Victoria's children marrying into the royal houses of nearly every major

European power. Although the English constitutional arrangement denied her official powers in foreign affairs, she ruled her family with an iron fist and used her influence in that realm as a persuasive power abroad.

During her reign, Victoria also played a crucial role in parliamentary politics by acting as a mediator between arriving and departing prime ministers. She was a popular ruler, but there were at least seven attempts on her life during her time as queen. She was a prolific writer and kept numerous diaries throughout her adult life; many of the 122 volumes survive to this day, though some were destroyed.

Queen Victoria was devastated when Albert died in 1861, and she wore only black as a symbol of her mourning the remainder of her life. She died on the Isle of Wight in 1901 at the age of eighty-one, and at the time of her death, that was the longest reign of any monarch, male or female. She had forty-two grandchildren, and some of her ancestors became reigning European monarchs, most notably Queen Elizabeth II.

Given Queen Victoria's record-making reign and the indelible stamp her persona left on the country, it is no wonder that nineteenth-century Britain is referred to as the Victorian era. There are countless public spaces in London named after her, and her ethics and personality are still synonymous with many aspects of British culture.[1]

SUSAN B. ANTHONY (1820–1906)

Susan B. Anthony was a leading feminist, human rights activist, abolitionist, reformer, teacher, and lecturer. She devoted her life to women's rights issues and helped abolish slavery. She campaigned widely for equal rights for women—namely for women to legally own their own property, retain the wages they worked for, and have access to education. She founded the American Equal Rights Association (AERA) and the National Woman Suffrage Association (NWSA). In 1900, she convinced the University of Rochester to admit women. She remained devoted to fighting for change until her death.

Susan B. Anthony devoted her life to two important causes affecting the United States: abolition and women's suffrage.

Anthony was raised in New York in a Quaker community and was immersed in the antislavery movement that Quakers began. She was a teacher for fifteen years at a Quaker seminary. When she was twenty-nine, she became actively involved in both the major reform causes sweeping the United States: the abolitionist movement and the temperance movement.

She became devoted to fighting for women's rights and campaigning for woman suffrage after meeting Elizabeth Cady Stanton, a fellow women's rights and abolitionist activist who would become her lifelong political partner. Stanton was married and had several children, and thus her ability to travel was limited. Since Anthony never married or had children, she was free to travel and present the passionate speeches Stanton wrote at home. As a result, Anthony became the face of women's rights, which also meant she was the object of much criticism from a public that favored patriarchal domination and was resistant to accepting women's rights.

After the Civil War, Anthony and Stanton organized to support the petition for the Thirteenth Amendment to outlaw slavery. They were extremely bitter and disappointed that women were excluded from the ratified amendments and still unable to legally vote. Anthony felt greatly discouraged that so many abolitionists and suffragists excluded women's rights from their fight for black rights. As a result, she founded the National Woman Suffrage Association with Stanton and Lucy Stone.

Anthony, like many other women's rights activists was opposed to abortion. Though not so odd for her time, but certainly odd for our current understanding of feminism, she firmly believed that women's rights to their own bodies and equal rights would end the need for abortion, and thus she used this stance to campaign for women's equality. Even though Anthony fought for the abolishment of slavery, some of Anthony's views were, unfortunately, also racist; she stated on more than one occasion that white women would be better voters than black men and recent immigrants. Her and Stanton's newspaper *Revolution*, even though it attacked lynch mobs and racial violence, was noted as espousing women rights before black rights. This may have been due to Anthony's frustration that the women's movement was put on hold in favor of abolition, but it soured many on her just the same. Anthony began campaigning for women's rights in 1853 and did not stop until her death at age eighty-six. In 1860, largely due to her efforts, the New York State Married Women's Property Bill was written into law. This law allowed women to own property, keep their own wages, and have legal custody of their children. Anthony continued to campaign across the nation for women's right to vote and was arrested in 1872 for voting in Rochester.

Susan B. Anthony retired as president of the NWSA in 1900, and she died in 1906. Though she worked tirelessly for women's suffrage, women were not granted the right to vote until 1920, when the Susan B. Anthony Amendment was finally added to the Constitution. In 1979, Anthony's image was placed on the new dollar coin, the first woman to be depicted on US currency.[2]

HARRIET TUBMAN (1820–1913)

Harriet Tubman is a true American hero. She escaped slavery and became one of the most important abolitionists in history. She later helped the radical abolitionist John Brown recruit men for his raid on Harpers Ferry, worked as an armed scout and spy for the United States Army, and was an outspoken leader for the women's suffrage movement. Using the famous Underground Railroad, she led hundreds of enslaved people to freedom in the North. Over a ten-year span, she made nineteen trips into the South. Despite the grave danger associated with the work of liberating slaves, Tubman bravely risked her own life repeatedly in order to help enslaved people reach freedom in Philadelphia. And, as she proudly stated to abolitionist and civil rights leader Frederick Douglass, she "never lost a single passenger."[3]

Former slave Harriet Tubman personally heped hundreds of people escape enslavement through the Underground Railroad.

Tubman was born into slavery in Dorchester County, Maryland, around 1820, and by age five she was working as a house servant. By age twelve, she was sent to work in the fields, and during this time she suffered an injury that would haunt her the rest of her life. Tubman incurred the injury by protecting another enslaved field hand against an angry overseer. The overseer threw a 2-pound (.9-kilogram) weight intended to strike the field hand, but Tubman stood in front to protect the person and was hit instead. The blow caused her to suffer seizures, deep sleep spells, visions, and headaches throughout her life.

Tubman married a free black man, John Tubman, in 1844, but little is known about the marriage. In 1849, she became ill again, and her value as a slave decreased. Her enslaver, Edward Brodess, tried to sell her, but due to her frail health he was unsuccessful. When Brodess died, Tubman worried about her future. Rather than suffer the fate of being put back on the market, she decided to escape the life of slavery she had been unjustly born into. Despite pleas from her husband to stay, she resolved to flee to Pennsylvania, a state that, unlike Delaware, had abolished slavery.

Tubman first escaped with two of her brothers in 1849, but they had second thoughts after seeing a runaway notice posted offering a $100 reward for their return, so they turned back and forced Tubman to return with them. But Tubman wouldn't be held down for long. She decided to escape again, this time aided by the Underground Railroad.

The Underground Railroad was not a literal railroad, but a secret resistance movement made up of abolitionists (activists who fought for the abolishment of the slave system) and their allies who were black and white, free and enslaved. The network was comprised of secret routes and safe houses to help enslaved fugitives reach the free states, and records suggest that by 1850, one hundred thousand slaves had escaped using the system. The Fugitive Slave Act of 1793 required officials from the free states to assist slaveholders and their bounty hunters in pursuit of runaway slaves, but many citizens and governments ignored this immoral law.

With great courage, Tubman set out on foot under the cover of night and followed the North Star making her way to Philadelphia, where she found freedom and work. She returned to Maryland and helped her sister and nieces escape, and then she made a perilous journey to the South to rescue her brother and two other men. Tubman returned to the South repeatedly, becoming a skilled resistance leader and helping enslaved fugitives reach the free states. She was such a threat that by 1856 the reward for Tubman's capture in the South was $40,000. She had gone to the South nineteen times by 1860, managing to rescue her entire family and parents and hundreds of others. In honor of her courage and effective efforts in leading fugitives to freedom, the prominent abolitionist William Lloyd Garrison nicknamed her "Moses" for her remarkable acts of bravery during such dangerous and life-endangering work. When the Civil War broke out in 1861, Tubman, like many others, saw the defeat of the Confederacy a necessary step in the abolition of slavery. When President Lincoln finally issued the Emancipation Proclamation—the executive order proclaiming all slaves free—in 1863, Tubman was determined to liberate all black men, women, and children from slavery. Working as a scout and a spy for the Union, Tubman became the first woman to lead an armed assault during the Civil War. She helped to rescue more than 750 enslaved people during the Combahee River raid. In her later years, Tubman was active in the women's suffrage movement alongside leaders Susan B. Anthony and Emily Howland. Tubman traveled to New York, Washington, D.C., and Boston to campaign for women's voting rights. She was also the keynote speaker for the National Federation of Afro-American Women in 1896.

Tubman, though widely known and recognized for her important work during her lifetime, became an icon after her death. She is one of the most famous and identifiable Americans. Countless schools and parks are named after her. In April 2016, the US Treasury announced that her image would be used on the $20 bill, replacing the slave-holding Andrew Jackson's portrait.

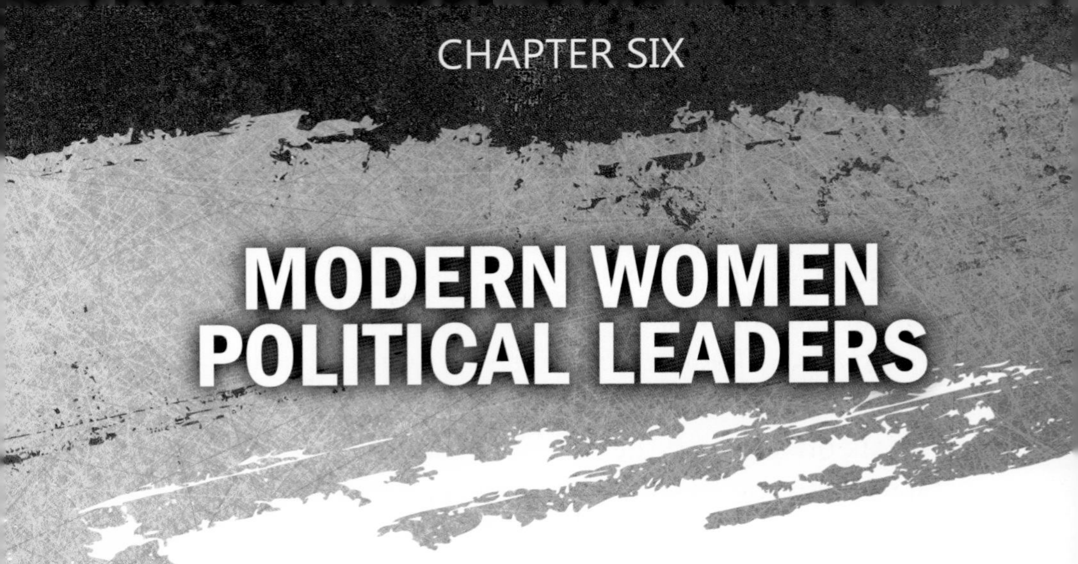

CHAPTER SIX

MODERN WOMEN POLITICAL LEADERS

The twentieth century marked the greatest change and advancements for women in America and Europe, though of course these advancements and opportunities also varied for individual women, depending on race and class. Thanks to the tireless campaigning of the suffragette movements in both Britain and America, by the second decade of the century, women gained the right to vote. World War II brought dramatic and rapid change in the social and economic roles of women: women were expected to both work and take care of the households while the men were off to war. After the war, the 1950s ushered in a time of ideological cold-war scare tactics, sexism, and Jim Crow racism. This regressive and oppressive cultural climate created a tremendous backlash, and by the 1960s, the women's liberation, human rights, and civil rights movements were mobilized and fighting for change.

This chapter gives the reader a spectrum of women from different races, nations, and economic stations who all were part of a movement for change. The women political leaders of the twentieth century set the stage for sexual and racial equality, and they continue to shatter gender barriers in the twenty-first century.

ELEANOR ROOSEVELT (1884–1962)

Eleanor Roosevelt changed the role of the First Lady of the United States through her work as a politician, diplomat, and human rights activist. She was the longest-serving First Lady, holding the post during her husband Franklin D. Roosevelt's four terms in office. She also served as the US delegate to the United Nations General Assembly and was the first chairperson of the Presidential Commission on the Status of Women under President John F. Kennedy's administration.

After her tenure as First Lady, Eleanor Roosevelt continued to serve the public. From 1946–1948, she helped draft the Universal Declaration of Human Rights.

Roosevelt was born in New York City and was the niece of former president Theodore Roosevelt. Her parents suffered from numerous ailments and addictions, and both died early of diphtheria, leaving her orphaned by age ten. Eleanor lived with her grandmother in Tivoli, New York. She was a shy, insecure girl who felt like an ugly duckling; however, even as a teenager she realized physical beauty was not the most important attribute to having a full life. At age fifteen, she was sent to a finishing school in England, and the experience helped draw her out of her shell. She wanted to stay longer, but when her education ended she returned to the United States to be presented at the debutante society ball held at the Waldorf Astoria hotel in New York City.

Eleanor married her distant cousin Franklin D. Roosevelt. The two had met on the train from New York City to Tivoli in 1902. They embarked on a secret romance and became engaged a year later. Although Franklin's mother, Sara, opposed the union, the two were married in 1905. They returned from their honeymoon and moved to Hyde Park, New York, residing in a house given to them by Franklin's mother. Eleanor had difficulty with her controlling mother-in-law, whose house was connected to theirs by sliding doors. Sara meddled in their affairs, including seeking control in raising the couple's six children. Eleanor suffered a breakdown and resented Sara's constant presence and controlling manner.

Eleanor did not take to marriage or motherhood easily. In 1918, she found love letters written by her husband to his secretary, Lucy Mercer. Franklin wanted to leave his wife for Mercer, but following pressure from his political advisor he did not. His mother also threatened to disinherit him should he break up his marriage. Yet the affair had an effect on the couple's relationship, transforming their marriage into more of a political partnership than a romantic union. Disillusioned with her husband and with marriage, Eleanor threw herself into public life and focused more on developing her social work skills rather than being a stay-at-home wife and mother.

In 1921 during a family vacation, Franklin contracted polio, a virus that permanently paralyzed his legs. After it was clear Franklin would never walk again, Sara and Eleanor became embroiled in a battle over his political future: Sara felt the proper thing to do would be for him to retire and stay out of the public eye given his disability, but Eleanor persuaded him to remain in politics. As Eleanor's own political work became more prominent, she became less influenced by the controlling will of her mother-in-law. Eleanor also had several close relationships with women outside of her marriage to Franklin, including legendary pilot Amelia Earhart and AP reporter Lorena Hickock.

When Franklin was elected president in 1933, Eleanor began her tenure as First Lady, a role she would dramatically alter. Unlike previous First Ladies, she refused to stay relegated to the domestic sphere and instead was active in fighting for a number of human rights issues. She fought for the rights of women and children and spoke out against poverty and racial oppression. She gave numerous press conferences and was highly active in shaping public policy. Due to her visibility as a powerful woman leader at a time when women did not have much opportunity to affect the public sphere, she was highly criticized by some. Yet today she is regarded as one of the most important leaders of women's and civil rights, as well as one of the earliest public officials to use the mass media to publicize important causes to effect societal change.

Franklin Roosevelt died in 1945, but that didn't end Eleanor's time in the public eye. She continued to fight for social causes during the administrations of presidents Truman and Kennedy. She also became chair of the UN Human Rights Commission and helped to write the Universal Declaration of Human Rights. Eleanor also wrote several books about her life and experiences, including *This Is My Story* (1937), *This I Remember* (1949), *On My Own* (1958), and *Autobiography* (1961).[1]

EVA PERON (1919–1952)

Eva Peron, otherwise known by the affectionate diminutive mononym "Evita," was Argentina's leading political figure and First Lady from 1946 until her death in 1952. In 1945, she married Juan Peron, a famous political leader. When he subsequently won the presidency of Argentina, she assumed the mantle of First Lady. As First Lady, Eva Peron amassed a loyal constituency through a combination of personal charisma, feminism, and dedication to improving life among the poor. She would eventually leverage this political capital into the founding of the Female Peronist Party, Argentina's first women's political party.

Born Maria Eva Duarte in 1919, she rose from humble origins. Her mother, Juana Ibarguren, and father, Juan Duarte, were not married. Duarte had a wife and family elsewhere. While this practice was not uncommon for rich rural Argentine men, Duarte did not adequately support his "second" family. In 1926, he died in a car accident, placing more financial stress on Eva's already poor family. In search of income, the family relocated to the nearby city of Junin, where they shared a small apartment and all found domestic work. However, Eva did not last long in this situation. She fled Junin for Buenos Aries at age fifteen.

Arriving in Depression-era Buenos Aries with little but her wits, Eva quickly realized her dream of being a professional actress. She landed a part in a play called *Mrs. Perez* and continued building a résumé with touring theater work, modeling, and some film roles. Her major break, however, would be in radio. In 1942, Eva was hired for a regular part on a daytime show called *Muy Bien*. Eva used this as a stepping-stone for more prestigious employment, which she found in the popular but more high-minded radio program, *Great Women of History*. In a role that foreshadowed her fate, she played iconic women in history such as Queen Elizabeth I and Catherine the Great.

Eva's life would soon change even more significantly. After a devastating earthquake killed ten thousand people, then Secretary of Labor Juan Peron organized an arts festival to benefit its victims. At the festival, he met Eva Duarte, and the two fell in love. Peron's political career was on the upswing, which his opponents countered by jailing him. This only increased his popularity and support, and with the help of labor unions, Peron was soon released from prison. Moved by Eva's support and loyalty, Peron married her in 1945. As it was unusual for a politician to marry a woman born poor and out of wedlock, the marriage conferred upon Eva a rise in social status.

The exceedingly popular first lady of Argentina, Eva Peron, greeted adoring crowds from her balcony.

Peron soon decided to seek the presidency. Usually at her husband's side on the campaign trail, Eva endeared herself to the nation, particularly women and the poor. Owing to her humble origins, Eva cultivated a credible populist persona. Peron won the 1946 presidential election by a large margin. The following year, Eva embarked on a grand tour of Europe, dubbed the Rainbow Tour. She met with several heads of state, including Francisco

Franco, the Fascist leader of Spain. Although the meeting was due to cultural affinities between the two countries, the meeting sowed the seeds of suspicion with regard to the Perons' ties to Fascism in Latin America.

Evita's most important enduring legacy is her work on behalf of feminism and women's suffrage. Although she did not actually draft the legislation, her vocal support helped pass Law 13,010, extending voting rights to women. Next, she organized the Female Peronist Party, technically a branch of her husband's Peronist Justicialist political party. By expanding the political umbrella to women, she helped him secure another victory in 1951. Due to declining health and opposition from the military, she had to abandon her hopes of winning the vice presidency, a bid that might have been successful.

Eva Peron died of cervical cancer on July 26, 1952, at the age of thirty-three. Amid a massive outpouring of public mourning, Peron was given a state funeral. Due to her untimely death, she became something of a legend. As the subject of the smash 1976 Andrew Lloyd Webber musical *Evita*, her international significance in popular culture increased even further. Although her fame was enormous, she had detractors as well. During her time in power she clashed with Argentina's military, and (unsubstantiated) allegations of Peron's ties to Fascism in Latin America have been advanced. Nonetheless, Eva Peron remains the most famous woman in the modern history of Argentina and the undisputed "spiritual leader" of the nation—arguably to this day.

In addition to her legacy as populist hero and icon for the nation of Argentina, Peron was also to some extent responsible for collapsing a rigid boundary between entertainment and politics, a distinction that Americas have taken for granted since the presidency of Ronald Reagan.[2]

WANGARI MAATHAI (1940–2011)

Wangari Maathai was an academic, political activist, and environmentalist from Kenya. Maathai founded the Green Belt Movement; served as Kenya's assistant minister of environment, natural resources, and wildlife; and in 2004 became the first African woman to be awarded the Nobel Peace Prize. In addition, she was a noted author of several books, as well as the first woman from East Africa to earn a PhD.

Maathai was born on April 1, 1940, in Ihithe, a small Kenyan farming village in the Nyeri District. At age eight, she began attending primary school. Although it was unusual for Kenyan girls to receive an education at that time, she proved an excellent student. Her studies continued at St. Cecilia's, a Catholic boarding school where she learned

English, converted to Catholicism, and eventually graduated at the top of her class. This gained her entry to the selective Loreto High School, Kenya's only Catholic high school.

During Maathai's formative years, Kenya was a British colony. The colony would not gain independence until the Independent Republic of Kenya was established in 1964. However, by the time Maathai completed high school in 1960, Britain's colonial rule of East Africa was drawing to a close. For this reason, Kenyan politicians sought to make sure a Western education would remain available to high-achieving Kenyan students. With the cooperation of then-senator John F. Kennedy, an initiative known as Airlift Africa received funding for this purpose. Through this program, about three hundred Kenyans, including Maathia, received scholarships to study in the United States.

Wangari Maathai was awarded the Nobel Peace Prize in 2004 for her leadership in Kenya's Green Belt Movement.

Maathai arrived in the unlikely locale of Kansas, studying biology at Mount St. Scholastica College and earning a bachelor's degree in 1964. She obtained a master's degree in biological sciences two years later at the University of Pittsburgh. After a brief stint studying in Germany, Maathai returned to Kenya and completed her PhD in veterinary anatomy at the University of Nairobi, becoming the first African woman to reach this level of education. By 1976, she was appointed chair of the Department of Veterinary Anatomy there, again becoming the first woman in this position.

Maathai's personal life during this time was turbulent. While pursuing her doctorate, Maathai met and married Mwangi Mathai. The couple had three children but later separated, allegedly because Maathai's independence and strong will were at odds with patriarchal Kenyan culture. Due to these persistent sexist attitudes, the divorce proceedings were complicated and even resulted in a brief stay in jail for Maathai. The divorce became official in 1979. However, onerous legal fees left her in dire straits financially, requiring her to leave academia.

The Green Belt Movement is perhaps Maathai's most enduring legacy. Years of colonialist economic policies exploited Kenya's natural resources, leaving the country's forests in ruin. To counter this, Maathai proposed the idea of community-based tree-planting projects. A secondary goal of the Green Belt Movement was the inclusion of women. The project was responsible for planting more than thirty million trees and taught women valuable skills, such as conservation and community organizing.

Maathai's political career advanced with a seat in the Kenyan Parliament, which she earned in 2002. She was subsequently appointed assistant minister of environment, natural resources, and wildlife. The culmination of her life's work as an environmentalist and political activist occurred in 2004 when she received the Nobel Peace Prize. In her acceptance speech she praised the idea that "peace" includes sustainability. In addition to her 2006 memoir, *Unbowed*, she wrote several books, notably *The Green Belt Experience: Sharing the Approach* and the *Experience* in 2004. Maathai succumbed to ovarian cancer at the age of seventy-one in 2011.[3]

INDIRA GANDHI (1917–1984)

Indira Gandhi is to date India's only female prime minister. Born into the prominent political family of Jawaharlal Nehru, India's first prime minister after independence from Britain, she served as the prime minister from 1966 to 1977. She resumed the post in 1980, until her assassination in 1984. After her father, she is the longest-serving prime minister of India. Gandhi was known for her political prowess and ruthlessness in her leadership. She obtained an unprecedented centralization of power and waged war on Pakistan in support of the independence movement, resulting in India's centrality on the South Asian political scene.

An only child, Gandhi had an unhappy and solitary childhood. Her father was a busy politician, and her mother was frequently ill. She was home tutored until she was sent away to a Swiss boarding school and did not have much contact with her father except through letters. Gandhi was highly intelligent and attended Oxford University, but she did not complete her studies. After her mother's death in 1936, her father leaned on Indira to help him host some of the world's most important political leaders. This position exposed her early to diplomacy, as she had to learn how to navigate the political world of her father.

Gandhi was elected president of the Indian National Congress in 1960 and appointed minister of information and broadcasting. She was elected prime minister after her father's successor died in 1966. Due in part to a war with Pakistan, Gandhi inherited a weak and struggling economy. Immediately taking to her role and seeking reform, she fired high-ranking officials and brought about significant changes in agricultural programs that benefited the poorest of the nation. Gandhi was hailed as a hero for these efforts, and her work also led to the creation of the independent nation of Bangladesh. She led the Green Revolution, addressing the dire food shortages by diversifying crops and increased food exports, thereby creating more food as well as jobs for impoverished citizens.

Indira Gandhi was India's first—and, to date, only—elected female prime minister. Although she is associated with corruption and authoritarianism, she advocated many programs to aid the poor.

Even with these advancements, Gandhi became increasingly more corrupt and ruled with an authoritarian hand, so much so that her opponents called for her resignation by 1975. To avoid losing her position, she had a state of emergency called so that she could continue her post, but she soon lost the next election and was imprisoned. Crippled by a struggling economy, the people elected her in 1980 by a landslide. It was during this time that the Sikh separatist movement fomented, and Gandhi attempted to repress it. In retaliation, Sikh extremists protested outside the Golden Temple. During this demonstration, Gandhi ordered thousands of soldiers to infiltrate the protest, and more than 450 people were killed.

In 1984, she was murdered by two trusted bodyguards who were Sikhs. Although Indira Gandhi is associated with corruption, authoritarianism, and nepotism, she also represents progressiveness in that she was the first woman elected to hold the office of prime minister of India. Delhi's Indira Gandhi International Airport and the Indira Gandhi National Open University are both named in her honor.[4]

MARGARET THATCHER (1925–2013)

Margaret Thatcher was the first, and to date the only, female prime minister of the United Kingdom.

Thatcher served from 1979 to 1990. During her time in office, she earned the nickname "Iron Lady" because much like her friend and ally at the time, US president Ronald Reagan, she was ideologically opposed to the Soviet Union. Thatcher also fought a small war with Argentina to control the Falkland Islands during her term, but her time in office is most characterized by her implementation of the privatization of industries and the scaling back of public benefits. She served longer than any other prime minister but was finally pressured into resigning by members of the Conservative Party.

Thatcher was born Margaret Roberts in 1925 in a small town, where her family owned a corner store. Her father, Alfred Roberts, was extremely influential on Margaret's worldview. He was a devoted Methodist and was rather strict, but he instilled in Margaret a stern work ethic and the values of public service. Alfred was also a politician who served on the town council for years. Winston Churchill, the prime minister during World War II, also inspired Margaret. Much like the rest of the country, she viewed his triumph over the Nazis and refusal to compromise as heroic.

Thatcher studied chemistry at the University of Oxford and was elected president of the students' Conservative Association. Although she began her career as a scientist at BX Plastics, she was eager to pursue politics and joined the Young

Conservatives. In 1950 she ran for Parliament as the youngest candidate in the Labor Party, using the slogan "Vote Right to Keep What's Left." Although she lost, she received more votes than previous candidates in her party. The following year, she married Dennis Thatcher, a wealthy businessman. The couple had twins shortly after their wedding. Thatcher faced frustration when she was not selected as a Conservative Party candidate to run in 1953, as some committees would not accept a young mother as their Parliament candidate. She studied for her bar exams and passed them in 1954.

Thatcher ran for Parliament once again in 1959 and won the seat. She introduced a bill that affirmed the right of media to cover local government meetings. In 1961, she accepted an invitation to become parliamentary undersecretary in the Ministry of Pensions and National Insurance. She moved up in Parliament, becoming secretary of state for education and science. When the Conservatives took power of Parliament in 1970, she was demonized for cutting back social welfare programs and public benefits. Her opponents in her own party called her "Thatcher the milk snatcher" after she cancelled the free milk program for schools. Despite these criticisms, she kept her job and in 1975 took over the Labor Party.

Thatcher became prime minister in 1979, at a time when the UK was in financial distress. She

The "Iron Lady," British Prime Minister Margaret Thatcher was criticized for her treatment of the working class. During her decade in office, she privatized many state-run companies, altering England's economic and social structure.

portrayed herself as practical housewife who could turn the country around. She promised the nation she would bring economic stability, and she championed free markets, arguing that individuals, not the government, should make their own success. During her first term, the government lowered individual taxes, sold off public housing for the poor, and put in austerity measures even as inflation and unemployment were rising. Her policies did not bring inflation or unemployment down, and summer riots broke out across urban centers. Polls showed that she was the most unpopular prime minister in recorded history.

In 1982, Argentina invaded the British-colonized Falkland Islands, and Thatcher dispatched troops to the area, refusing to give over control. Argentina surrendered after ten weeks of fighting, and this victory won Thatcher worldwide popularity. Her radical economic policies were also changing the face of Britain. Her rhetoric of individualism and personal responsibility was familiar in a nation like the United States, but not so in the UK. She privatized public housing and former state-run utility companies like the British Rail, British Telecommunications, and British Gas. The economy boomed, but as in the United States, inequality and homelessness increased.

In 1984, Thatcher refused to meet the demands of the striking miners' union. Thatcher held firm for twelve months, refusing to negotiate with the union, until it conceded defeat and the miners returned to work. Although her party and the establishment supported her actions, she became a figure of contempt among many working-class and left-leaning communities.

Thatcher was elected to a third term in 1987, and she soon implemented the poll tax, which created disputes across Europe. Experiencing rapid unpopularity, she lost support in her own party and was challenged by former defense secretary Michael Heseltine. Betrayed, she resigned from her position as prime minister in 1990. Thatcher resigned completely from Parliament in 1992, and she died in 2013.

The biographical and controversial film *The Iron Lady* (2011) depicts Thatcher's political rise and fall. Even today she remains a controversial figure. Supporters see her as saving the United Kingdom from economic disaster by privatizing many state-run programs and eliminating public benefits, while critics see her as emblematic of a conservative culture created to benefit the wealthy and as someone who destroyed the livelihoods of working-class men and women during her tenure.[5]

GRACE LEE BOGGS (1915–2015)

Grace Lee Boggs was an activist, feminist, philosopher, writer, and scholar. During her long life, Boggs participated in nearly every major movement in the United States spanning the past century: civil rights, labor rights, women's rights, black power, and environmental justice. Her autobiography, *Living for Change* (1998), is taught in university classrooms; it documents her lifetime of activism and the social movements she helped forge while striving for justice for oppressed and marginalized people in the United States.

Born to first-generation Chinese immigrants, Grace Lee received a BA from Barnard College in 1935 and a PhD in philosophy from Bryn Mawr College in 1940. She faced significant barriers in the academic world of the 1940s, a climate that was hostile to women, and especially women of color. After earning her doctorate, Grace met and worked with the famous West Indian Marxist C.L.R. James and became active in the African American community, where she met fellow activist James Boggs. She married Boggs and moved to Detroit in 1953, where she remained working for change until she died.

In the 1960s, Grace and James became members of the black power movement and often hosted Malcolm X when he was in Detroit. Initially, Boggs believed strongly in the black power movement as a more pragmatic approach to equal rights, viewing Martin Luther King Jr.'s nonviolent strategies as ineffective and naïve. Yet in 1967, when race riots exploded in Detroit and across the nation, Boggs saw King's pacifism

Activist and philosopher Grace Lee Boggs challenged the power structure in America, particularly in Detroit. During her long life, Boggs was active in the feminist, Black Power, and civil rights movements, among many others.

as a better way to achieve cultural revolution, and she grew to feel the absence of a spiritual dimension was problematic in the black power movement. Boggs was particularly influenced by King's concept of the Beloved Community. Boggs, like King, believed in realizing a global vision in which all people can share the wealth of the earth and where poverty, hunger, racism, bigotry, discrimination, and homelessness would be eradicated and peace and justice could prevail over war and conflict. She dedicated her life to the effort of realizing King's vision of the Beloved Community in Detroit.

Boggs founded Detroit Summer in 1992, a multicultural intergenerational youth program and recipient of numerous awards. She is the subject of the documentary *The American Revolutionary: The Evolution of Grace Lee Boggs* (2013), and in 2014, the New School's University Center was named the Baldwin Rivera Boggs Center after activists James Baldwin, Sylvia Rivera, and Grace Lee Boggs. She died in 2015 at the age of one hundred.[6]

ANGELA DAVIS (1944–)

Angela Davis is a political activist, writer, and educator. Born on January 26, 1944, in Birmingham Alabama, Davis is best known for her civil rights and feminist activism during the 1960s and 1970s. She has also maintained a long and distinguished career as a speaker, scholar, and professor. Known internationally for her ongoing work to fight oppression in the United States and abroad, Davis is a living witness to the historical struggles of the contemporary era. Davis has lectured in more than fifty countries and has written numerous books on civil, feminist, and prison rights. She received the honor of being awarded an appointment to the University of California Presidential Chair in African American and Feminist Studies in 1994.

Davis was born in the "Dynamite Hill" area of Birmingham, Alabama, where racial discrimination was a systematic threat. The middle-class neighborhood earned the nickname because so many African Americans' homes were bombed by the racist white supremacist group the Ku Klux Klan. Davis's father, Frank, was a service station owner, and her mother, Sallye, was an elementary school teacher and an active member of the National Association for the Advancement of Colored People (NAACP) during the Jim Crow era, a time when it was extremely dangerous to be openly associated with civil rights organizations. Sallye Davis decided to pursue a master's degree at NYU and took teenaged Angela to New York City with her. Davis attended Elizabeth Irwin High School, where many of teachers were active communists who had been blacklisted during the McCarthy era. As a teenager, Davis organized interracial study groups, which were broken up by the police.

Davis enrolled in Brandeis University in 1961, where she was one of only three black students. Initially feeling alienated, Davis soon befriended foreign students and decided to major in French.

During a rally, she met the influential Frankfurt School philosopher Herbert Marcuse, whom became Davis's mentor. In a 2007 television interview, she said, "Herbert Marcuse taught me that it was possible to be an academic, an activist, a scholar, and a revolutionary."[7] During her time at Brandeis, Davis spent one year at the Sorbonne. She earned a B.A. in French in 1965 but decided her true interest was philosophy. After studying in Germany at the University of Frankfurt for two years, she followed her mentor Marcuse to finish her degree and earned her M.A. from the University of California at San Diego in 1968. Davis joined the Student Nonviolent Coordinating Committee (SNCC) and the Black Panther Party by 1967, and in 1968 she became a member of the American Communist Party.

Despite offers from Princeton and Swarthmore, Davis accepted a position of assistant professor of philosophy in 1969 from the University of California in Los Angeles, due to its urban location. By this time, Davis was well known as a radical feminist and a member of the Communist Party and Black Panther Party. Governor Ronald Reagan urged the Board of Regents to fire her for her radical politics and involvement in the Communist Party. Judge Jerry Pacht ruled that the regents could not fire

Davis solely because of her affiliations with the Communist Party, and Davis resumed her post only to be released again in June 1970, when the regents fired her for using offensive language.

During the early 1970s, Davis also fought hard to improve prison conditions for inmates. Her campaign to release the Soledad Brothers from unjust incarceration gained national attention and led to her own arrest and incarceration.

Educator, activist, and writer Angela Davis was once placed on the FBI's Ten Most Wanted list. Davis has spoken out against the prison industrial complex, advocating for more resources to be spent on education than on prison.

The Soledad Brothers were members of the Black Panther Party who were incarcerated in the late 1960s, charged with killing a prison guard at Soledad Prison.

In 1970, a seventeen-year-old black man named Jonathan Jackson gained control of a courtroom in Marin County using a shotgun. The police fired, and when all was said and done, the judge and three black men were killed, with several others injured. The firearms used in the attack were traced to Angela Davis, leading to a nationwide attempt to arrest her. FBI director J. Edgar Hoover listed her on the FBI's Ten Most Wanted Fugitives List. Davis fled California, but FBI agents found her in a motel in New York City. On January 5, 1971, Davis declared her innocence of all charges leveled against her in front of the court and nation. While awaiting trial, Davis was unfairly placed in solitary confinement in the Women's Detention Center. Across the nation, thousands of people began organizing a movement to free Angela Davis. By February 1971, more than two hundred local committees in the United States and sixty-seven in foreign countries worked to free Davis from prison. In 1972, after a sixteen-month incarceration, the state allowed her release on bail from county jail. Davis was tried, and the all-white jury found her not guilty. The fact that she owned the gun used in the crime was not enough evidence to establish her responsibility for the courtroom murders.

Davis remains an advocate of prison abolition and continues to wage a powerful critique of racism in the criminal justice system. She is a founding member of Critical Resistance, a national organization dedicated to ending the prison industrial complex. During the last three decades, Davis has lectured in all fifty of the United States, as well as in Africa, Cuba, Europe, the Caribbean, and the former USSR. Her articles and essays have been published in numerous academic journals and anthologies, and she is the author of nine books, including the influential *Women, Race and Class* and her best-selling autobiography, *Angela Davis: An Autobiography*. Her influence on feminist leaders and for all of those fighting oppression around the globe is invaluable.

MALALA YOUSAFZAI (1997–)

Malala Yousafzai is a Pakistani activist and advocate for girls' education. From a very young age, she consistently spoke out against the Taliban's denial of young women's access to education, resulting in a death threat against her. In 2012, she was shot in the head by Taliban operatives. Despite sustaining critical injuries, Yousafzai made a full

Malala Yousafzai's bravery, intelligence., and grace thrust her into the international spotlight as a young girl, Her efforts to promote and facilitate educational opportunities for women around the world earned her the Nobel Peace Prize.

recovery, and she emerged as an even more powerful voice for universal education. In 2014, Yousafzai won the Nobel Peace Prize, becoming the youngest-ever recipient of the award.

Malala Yousafzai was born into a Sunni Muslim family in the city of Mingora on July 12, 1997. Mingora is the largest municipality in the Swat District, a region in the Khyber Pakhtunkhwa Province of Pakistan, popular with tourists and known for its beautiful scenery, including mountains, lakes, and meadows. Malala's father, Ziauddin, owned and operated a local school and also wrote poetry on the side. He encouraged his daughter's love of learning and political consciousness, even allowing her to take part in late-night political discussions.

Malala's peaceful, comfortable early life enabled her intellectual development. However, in 2007, the Taliban seized control of much of northwestern Pakistan, including the Swat Valley, ending a relatively long period of stability. The Taliban instituted repressive policies, banning girls from going to school and prohibiting most forms of culture and media. These policies were backed with violent tactics such as suicide attacks and bombings. Perhaps worst of all, the Taliban destroyed hundreds of schools and laid waste to historic Buddhist artifacts. For a young woman with a strong set of liberal convictions, including a passionate belief in education, this state of affairs was intolerable.

With the support of her father, Malala decided to take action. In 2008, the precocious eleven-year-old went to Peshawar to deliver a talk titled "How Dare the Taliban Take Away My Basic Right to Education," which aired on

Pakistani television. Soon after, Malala began publishing her diary entries for an Urdu-language blog administered by the British Broadcasting Corporation (BBC). Her first entry was titled "I Am Afraid" and revealed nightmares of escalating violence. This and subsequent posts expressed much anxiety and trepidation, as well as anger, about daily life under Taliban rule. Due to the danger of expressing these views, Malala adopted the pseudonym of Gul Makai. However, her real identity was revealed later that year. Due to approaching war between Pakistan and the Taliban, Malala was forced to flee the Swat District, becoming an internally displaced person (IDP) in May of 2009.

After her brief relocation, Malala returned to her home and commenced her advocacy for young women's basic right to a free, quality education. Her rising profile earned her a nomination for the International Children's Peace Prize in 2011. Later that year, Malala was awarded Pakistan's National Youth Peace Prize. Despite being issued a death threat, she continued to attend school, primarily because it was assumed that the Taliban would not actually carry out such a threat on a young woman.

Such optimism proved unfounded. On October 9, 2012, two Taliban members stopped a school bus. One boarded and demanded to know which girl was Malala. After her classmates turned toward her to reveal her location, the gunman fired three shots, seriously wounding Malala and injuring two other girls. Malala was airlifted to a military hospital and then transferred to an intensive care unit in the United Kingdom.

After an astounding but protracted recovery, Malala began attending school in Birmingham, England, where she currently resides. The immense outpouring of support for her travails increased her profile globally. In 2013, she published an autobiography, *I Am Malala: The Girl Who Stood Up for Education and Was Shot by the Taliban*.

The following year, she established the Malala Fund with her father. Through this organization she traveled to Jordan, Kenya, and Nigeria, fostering a common cause with similarly oppressed woman and refugees beyond her own national borders. In October 2014, her efforts culminated in the Nobel Peace Prize. Malala accepted the award on behalf of all the "forgotten children who want education."[8]

Malala Yousafzai remains a steadfast voice for education advocacy. The Malala Fund currently operates in six countries, pursuing a number of projects all seeking to secure quality secondary education for girls.

HILLARY RODHAM CLINTON (1947–)

Hillary Rodham Clinton rose to fame as First Lady during husband Bill Clinton's two presidential terms, from 1993 to 2000. She went on to serve as a US senator and as secretary of state.

Hillary Rodham was born in Chicago. As a young woman she was active in young Republican groups, and in 1964, she campaigned for Barry Goldwater. Clinton became a Democrat in 1968. She attended Wellesley College and was elected senior class president. She graduated in 1969, and then attended Yale Law School, where she met Bill Clinton. She graduated with honors in 1973 and then completed one year of post-graduate study at the Yale Child Study Center, where she took courses on pediatric medicine. Politically active, she worked on Walter Mondale's subcommittee on migrant workers, and she also campaigned for Democratic presidential nominee George McGovern during her summers off from college. Hillary married Bill Clinton in 1975 and worked on President Jimmy Carter's campaign in 1976, the same year her husband was elected attorney general of Arkansas.

After President Nixon resigned, both Hillary and Bill Clinton became members of the Arkansas Law School faculty. Bill was elected governor, and Hillary served as First Lady of the state from 1979

While Hillary Clinton's list of accomplishments is long, she has endured more than her share of scrutiny and sexist attitudes. Clinton made history by becoming the first woman to be nominated for president by a major political party.

to 1992. She also served on the boards of TCBY and Wal-Mart. Bill Clinton was elected to the presidency in 1992, and Hillary proved a valuable—and controversial—First Lady. She was head of the Task Force on National Health Reform in 1993, but the health care plan was abandoned in 1994. As First Lady, Hillary endured several scandals. First, she and her husband became embroiled in the Whitewater real estate project, an ordeal that cost the government $73 million. Then, in 1998, President Clinton was impeached for a sex scandal. The Senate did not convict President Clinton, and he remained in office, but the ordeal momentarily took a toll on his reputation. Although Hillary publicly supported her husband during this highly publicized affair, she did privately contemplate ending her marriage.

Clinton sought the New York State Senate seat. With her election, she became the first First Lady to win a public office and also the first woman to win a New York Senate seat. In 2007 she announced she would run for the presidency, seeking to be the first female US president. After a tough primary campaign, she conceded to Barack Obama. President Obama appointed Clinton secretary of state in 2009. She made human rights and women's rights a central concern, and she also led the United States diplomatic efforts in the

Middle East. A successful tenure in the position was almost tarnished by scandal when Clinton came under investigation for attacks made on the US embassy in Bengazi, Libya, in 2012. Allegations were made that Clinton knew of the plan for the attack and was ineffectual in preventing it, but she denied this. She resigned from her post in 2013.

Clinton announced she would run for US presidency again in 2015. She secured the Democratic Party nomination in 2016, becoming the first woman to earn the nomination for a major party's presidential bid. Like Obama, Clinton is passionate about lowering student debt and improving the Obamacare health program, as well as about women's rights. Yet Clinton has also come under considerate criticism for changing her stances on issues like gay marriage, which she did not support in 2008 but now does. She is also known to support fracking, a controversial way to procure natural gas. Clinton published a best selling memoir, *Hard Choices*, in 2014.[9]

CONCLUSION

While it would be inadvisable to posit a set of essential, transhistorical characteristics shared by female political leaders across disparate epochs and cultures, we will nevertheless conclude our survey by identifying a few important traits notable women political leaders hold in common. Although we might identify similarities between these women in terms of their respective paths to power and political ideals, it is important to resist any totalizing generalizations about female political leadership.

Foremost, and perhaps most obviously, all female leaders have ascended to power within patriarchal political spheres—though in quite different ways. Upper-class women such as Eleanor of Aquitaine and Catherine de Medici leveraged their vast inherited wealth into politically advantageous marriages. In such instances, proximity to the throne and skillful navigation of birthrights landed these women in charge, sometimes first as acting regents, but subsequently as legitimate heads of state with firm mandates to rule. Contrastingly, women of lower economic and social status have had comparatively limited avenues through which to channel their political skills and instincts. This is not to vilify ambition or upward mobility in women, but rather to suggest that in societies stratified by class and gender, women are forced to work within adversarial power structures to actualize their political will, and they have done so successfully. Although these female rulers rarely if ever transcend patriarchy, it can be argued that firsthand knowledge of how patriarchal power functions increased their political acumen and efficacy.

Moreover, perhaps due to some identification with the comparatively less powerful in male-dominated societies (which nearly all societies have been), female rulers have often favored progressive reforms within their respective political worlds. Of course, this has not always been the case. The fiscally conservative Queen Isabella of Spain presided over the Spanish Inquisition. Centuries later, Margaret Thatcher would dismantle much of England's social safety net in the name of the so-called free market. In the election season of 2016, Hillary Clinton embodied this uneasy tension. Some saw her as nothing more than a corporate shill and the epitome of establishment politics, others as a champion for equal pay, women's reproductive rights, and a living wage. Only time will tell which version of Clinton will take precedence in the history books.

Finally, in much of the developing world, the political status of women lags painfully behind that of men. Sectarian and ethnic violence, religious fundamentalism, and corporate exploitation threaten to make this worse. Under these conditions, brave women have spoken up for basic human rights such as health care and education and have been met with retaliatory threats, repression, and even gunfire. While women in the West have made great strides toward an articulate political voice, the adage that "injustice anywhere is a threat to freedom everywhere" remains true.

CHAPTER NOTES

CHAPTER 1. WOMEN LEADING IN ANCIENT TIMES

1. Wolfram Grajetzki, *Ancient Egyptian Queens: A Hieroglyphic Dictionary* (London, UK: Golden House, 2011).
2. History.com, "Nefertiti," http://www.history.com/topics/ancient-history/nefertiti (accessed April 25, 2016).
3. Ibid.
4. Chip Brown, "Hatshepsut," *National Geographic*, April 2010, http://ngm.nationalgeographic.com/2009/04/hatshepsut/brown-text/1 (accessed May 1, 2016).
5. Stacey Schiff, *Cleopatra: A Life* (New York, NY: Little & Brown Co., 2011).
6. Chip Brown, "The Search for Cleopatra," *National Geographic*, July 2011, http://ngm.nationalgeographic.com/print/2011/07/cleopatra/brown-text (accessed May 5, 2016).

CHAPTER 2. WOMEN LEADERS OF THE MIDDLE AGES

1. Paulo Cesaretti, *Theodora: Empress of Byzantium* (New York, NY: Vendome Press, 2012).
2. Ann Kramer, *Eleanor of Aquitaine: The Queen Who Rode Off to Battle* (Washington DC: National Geographic Society, 2006).

CHAPTER 3. WOMEN OF THE RENAISSANCE

1. Alison Weir, *Queen Isabella: Treachery, Adultery, and Murder in Medieval England*. (New York, NY: Ballantine Books, 2006).
2. Leona Frieda, *Catherine de Medici: Renaissance Queen of France* (New York, NY: Harper Perennial, 2006).
3. J. E. Neale, *Queen Elizabeth I: The Classic Biography of the Great Tudor Queen* (Chicago, IL: Academy of Chicago Press, 2001).

CHAPTER 4. WOMEN LEADING DURING THE ENLIGHTENMENT

1. Francine Du Plessix Gray, *Madame de Stael: The First Modern Woman* (New York, NY: W.W. Norton & Co., 2008).
2. Claire Tomalin, *The Life and Death of Mary Wollstonecraft* (New York, NY: Penguin Books, 1996).
3. Robert Massie, *Catherine the Great: Portrait of a Woman* (New York, NY: Random House, 2012).

CHAPTER 5. THE VICTORIAN, CIVIL WAR, AND RECONSTRUCTION ERAS

1. A. N. Wilson, *Queen Victoria: A Life* (New York, NY: Penguin Books, 2014).
2. Lynn Sherr, *Failure Is Impossible: Susan B Anthony*

in Her Own Words (New York, NY: Random House, 1995).

3. Catherine Clinton, *Harriet Tubman: The Road to Freedom* (New York, NY: Little, Brown & Company, 2014).

CHAPTER 6. MODERN WOMEN POLITICAL LEADERS

1. Maurine Hoffman Beasely, *Eleanor Roosevelt: The Transformative First Lady* (Lawrence, KS: University of Kansas Press, 2010).
2. James Barnes, *Evita, First Lady: The Biography of Eva Peron* (New York, NY: Grove Press, 1978).
3. Wangari Maathai, *Unbowed: A Memoir* (New York, NY: Random House, 2007).
4. Katherine Frank, *Indira: The Life of Indira Nehru Gandhi* (New York, NY: Harper Collins, 2010).
5. Jonathan Atikin, *Margaret Thatcher: The Power and Personality* (London, UK: Bloomsbury, 2013).
6. Grace Lee Boggs, *Living for Change: An Autobiography* (Minneapolis, MN: University of Minnesota Press, 1998).
7. Angela Davis, *Angela Davis: An Autobiography* (New York, NY: Random House, 1974).
8. Malala Yousafzai, *I Am Malala Yousafzai: The Story of How One Girl Stood Up for Education and Changed the World* (New York, NY: Little & Brown, 2014).
9. Hillary Rodham Clinton, *Hard Choices* (New York, NY: Simon & Schuster: 2014).

GLOSSARY

abolitionist One engaged in the act of eliminating an undesired social system. In America, the term is synonymous with the abolition of slavery.

ancient world Denotes the various societies around the Mediterranean and Near East from early civilization through the fall of the Roman Empire in 476 CE. Sometimes referred to as "antiquity."

ascension The act of formally rising to a seat of power in a monarchy. Often accompanied by a coronation.

Atenism Monotheistic religious movement started by Egyptian pharaoh Amenhotep IV in which traditional polytheistic deities were replaced by a single god of the sun.

Byzantine Relating to Byzantium or the Byzantine Empire.

Church of England Although established earlier, the Church of England is important because of its break with papal authority. This occurred when Henry VIII wished to annul his marriage, against Roman Catholic law.

consort Spouse of a reigning monarch.

duke A male holding hereditary authority in British and other European peerages.

Elizabethan Era Half century marked by the reign of Queen Elizabeth I, from 1558 to 1603.

Enlightenment A movement of the late seventeenth and eighteenth centuries in Europe emphasizing reason and science over tradition and authority.

Hellenistic Relating to Greek history, language, and culture, from the death of Alexander the Great to the suicides of Cleopatra and Mark Antony.

line of succession Hereditary rules governing who will ascend the throne after the death of a king or queen. This is an early system by which patriarchy was institutionalized.

Middle Ages The period of European history from the fall of the Roman Empire in the West (fifth century) to the fall of Constantinople (1453), or, more narrowly, from circa 1100 to 1453.

patriarchy Dominant order of male dominance through ingrained behavior, ideology, and social systems and institutions.

regent A person appointed to administer a country because the monarch is a minor or is absent or incapacitated.

Renaissance Cultural rebirth in Europe from the fourteenth century through the middle of the seventeenth century, based on the rediscovery of the classical literature.

throne A ceremonial chair for a monarch, used interchangeably with the abstract concept of power.

Tudor The English royal dynasty that held the throne from the accession of Henry VII in 1485 until the death of Elizabeth I in 1603.

Underground Railroad A system and route for allowing escaped slaves to escape to freedom in the North or Canada.

Victorian Of or relating to the reign of Queen Victoria.

FURTHER READING

BOOKS

Cooney, Kara. *The Woman Who Would Be King: Hatshepsut's Rise to Power in Ancient Egypt*. New York, NY: Crown Publishing Group, 2014.

Genovese, Michael A., and Janie S. Steckenrider. *Women as Political Leaders: Studies in Gender and Governing*.New York, NY: Routledge, 2013.

Lockhart, Michele, and Kathleen Mollick. *Global Women Leaders: Studies in Feminist Political Rhetoric*. London, UK: Lexington Books, 2014.

Massie, Robert K, *Catherine the Great: Portrait of a Woman*. New York, NY: Random House, 2011.

Matthai, Wangari. *Unbowed: A Memoir*. New York, NY: Alfred A. Knopf, 2006.

Pratt, Mary K. *Elizabeth I: English Renaissance Queen*. Edina, MN: ABDO, 2012.

Yousafzai, Malala. *I Am Malala: The Girl Who Stood Up for Education and Was Shot by the Taliban*. London, UK: Weidenfeld & Nicolson, 2013.

WEBSITES

Biography.com Notable Female Leaders
www.biography.com/people/groups/famous-female-leaders
Quick sketches of history's most important women leaders.

History and Theory of Feminism
www.gender.cawater-info.net/knowledge_base/rubricator/feminism_e.htm
Provides background on the history of feminism, from first-wave to the present.

National Democratic Institute
www.ndi.org/gender-women-democracy
This page explains why women's participation in politics and government is so important.

Women in the Ancient World
www.womenintheancientworld.com
This site examines the status, role, and daily life of women in the ancient civilizations in Egypt, Rome, Greece, and Israel.

INDEX

S

T

U

V

W

Y